ALSO BY ELIZA BOYD

A NEW LEASH ON LOVE

TRUE LOVE ANIMAL SANCTUARY #1

ELIZA BOYD

1

"Wow," Hannah Lockhart said, her voice breathy with awe. She peered around the twelve-acre property her cousin Brooke had purchased, her hands on her hips. "It's exactly like you pictured it."

Brooke nodded beside her, an unshakeable smile spreading across her face. She hadn't stopped since Hannah had arrived thirty minutes earlier. "It really is. From Stella's barn to the horse stables for future horses. Even to the pig pens—it's perfect, isn't it?"

The animal sanctuary *was* perfect. Pride swirled in Hannah's chest over what her cousin had accomplished in such a short amount of time. The idea had started percolating years ago, but after several setbacks, she'd thought Brooke might give up and try something else.

Ah, but no. That's not Brooke's style, and Hannah should have known better.

She also should have predicted that her cousin would build her sanctuary in a town called True Love. That screamed Brooke all over the place.

With Brooke's flowy maxi skirt, pixie haircut, and beaded bracelets lining her arms, Hannah wondered if this place would work out for her. Brooke had never been the small-town type, but if anyone could adapt, it was her cousin.

Hannah on the other hand? No way.

At the very least, she wanted a Target closer than thirty miles. She'd prefer a Whole Foods, but she'd take a well-known grocery chain with a decent natural living section in a pinch. After thirty minutes in this town, which she could have missed off I-40 if she'd blinked, she didn't think that this was the place for her.

But she'd happily help her cousin finish up the final prep so animals could be saved. It was temporary for her. Two weeks. Then she'd have to go back to her clients. Her job. Her home.

For now, she'd work during her downtime. Helping with the sanctuary would take up a lot of her time, but she couldn't completely drop the ball on her job. That was the beauty of being self-employed—she could work anywhere, anytime.

Limiting herself was hard, but that's why she'd taken her cousin up on her offer.

More like her request. Whatever. Either way, she was happy to do it.

The summer sun's heat licked at Hannah's bare shoulders. "Your tiny house has air conditioning, right?" She fanned herself with her hand, hoping against hope that the answer was yes.

With a light laugh, Brooke replied, "It does, and I'm thankful for that today. It's been unusually warm here this summer, I've heard."

"I wonder what that means for the winter."

Brooke turned to Hannah and lifted an eyebrow. "Thinking about staying?" she asked, folding her arms over her chest.

Hannah scoffed at that. "You know I'm not."

But Brooke didn't seem to take those words at face value. "We'll see about that."

Rolling her eyes, Hannah headed toward Stella's small field. Emerald grass gleamed right up to the rough trunks of shade trees. Underneath one, Hannah found Stella and gave the cow a few gentle strokes of her hand. "Tell your human mom that she isn't having one of those 'feelings' she thinks she has."

"When am I wrong though?" Brooke replied, coming over to the cow too. She wrapped her arms around her black-and-white body the best she could, seeing as Brooke was tiny compared to the thousand-pound animal. "I wasn't wrong about you coming here, about *me* coming here, or about making this sanctuary dream come true. And," she said, slipping away from the animal and facing her cousin, "I wasn't wrong about Jack."

Before Hannah said something she couldn't take back, she bit her tongue. She kept her ace card—the fact that Brooke had been wrong about her relationship with Teddy—in her back pocket. "That was a long time ago."

"Which is why I'm glad you're here. You've needed a fresh start and a break from work for a while now."

"So you asked me to come here for a different kind of work?" Hannah's forehead crinkled in her confusion.

"Yes!" Brooke exclaimed, stretching her hands down in a huff. "This isn't work for money's sake. This is work to make the world a better place."

"I do that with my work though. Coaching people improves their lives, which improves the world."

"You still need a break."

Hannah took a deep breath, letting her cousin's words sink in. She guessed Brooke had a point, so she'd chalk that feeling up as one in the "right" column. "What's on the agenda first, then?" she said, a hint of defeat in her voice.

That didn't deter Brooke. She clapped her hands excitedly and then waved one of them to have Hannah follow her. "We'll start with getting you something to eat. After your flights, I'm sure you're starving."

That was yet another feeling Brooke had gotten right. Hannah's stomach had been rumbling for at least the last hour. She'd packed snacks for her travel time, but real food would hit the spot.

Ten minutes later, they were in front of a diner that looked straight out of the 1950s.

"This is where you're taking me?" Hannah asked, disbelief tingeing her words.

Brooke got out of the car and marched toward the front door. "Yep. It's really the only choice, but I promise it won't disappoint."

Hannah wasn't so sure about that. At all. Diner food didn't really get along with her stomach. By real food, she'd thought about vegetables, whole grains, maybe some beans. Not greasy French fries and pancakes served all day.

As she followed behind her cousin, the juice bar across the street caught her eye. The sign above the door read *Main Squeeze - Juiced With Love*, which she thought seemed odd. But she remembered what the town was called, and as she read the rest of the shops' names, she recognized the running theme.

Ever After, the bookstore.

Brewing Affection, the coffee shop.

True Love Blooms, the florist.

Blushing Bridal, the bridal store.

Inn True Love, the inn the sanctuary shared property with.

Everything in this town was about love—the one thing she'd given up years ago.

Somehow, she kept her sigh to herself. This was the last

place she needed to be. She'd help her cousin and then get back home to Vermont. Pronto.

"Hey," she said to catch Brooke's attention. Then she pointed to the juice bar. "What about over there?"

"Oh, yeah. That's Luke's place. I've been there a couple of times, but it's really just juice and salads."

Lo and behold, Hannah was a salad girl. Not because she needed to diet or felt like she always had to watch her figure. She genuinely liked greens, veggies, and a good dressing. The idea had her mouth watering more than burgers and milkshakes would.

Even she knew how strange that was, but everyone was different.

And although this town didn't have a Whole Foods, at least *someone* was health conscious like she was. A juice bar was right up her alley.

"That sounds much more my speed," she told Brooke as she made a beeline across the street. No cars were stopped at the stop sign, and when she checked the name of the intersection, she nearly laughed.

Heart Street and Soul Road.

Heart and Soul.

Wow, this place was a lot. She had to leave as soon as she finished helping at the sanctuary.

Two weeks tops.

After swinging the door to the juice bar open, Hannah let out a sigh of relief. Air conditioning flew from the vents and cooled her down immediately, and she swore she could smell salad. But all of that meant very little the moment her eyes landed on the man behind the counter.

With a backwards cap, a white T-shirt, and three-day-old scruff on his face, the guy made it feel like the air conditioner had broken. Where'd the cool air go? Why did it feel like Arizona *inside* the small restaurant?

She didn't want to believe that it had anything to do with the man in front of her. Brooke, however, bumped her shoulder as if to say she was having one of her "feelings" about the matter.

"Hey, Luke," Brooke said to him.

Tersely, he nodded.

Brooke peeked at Hannah before looking back at him. "Luke Steiner, this is my cousin, Hannah Lockhart. She's helping out at the sanctuary for a while."

Again, all he did was nod.

What? No friendly wave or question about her cousin's sanctuary? So far, the town called True Love wasn't living up to its name.

"Know what you want?" the man asked, a little impatience ringing out.

Hannah cleared her throat and stepped forward, checking the menu out. They offered lots of juices and a few salads that sounded refreshing. Just what she needed after her travels.

"Are any of your dressings vegan *and* gluten-free?" she asked, keeping her eyes glued to the blackboard above his head. If she looked at him again, she'd start believing what Brooke had told her about this town.

"Everyone falls in love here. Seriously, everyone. They find their true love in this town—no exceptions."

Hannah had tried to tell Brooke that she'd be included in that if she moved there, but Brooke had insisted that the animals were her true love. The sanctuary would be all she needed. Not believing that for a second, Hannah had wanted to tell her that her feeling was totally off. She hadn't though, and now, she was glad. After she'd also insisted that she'd be immune when she visited, Brooke would be fast to throw this in her face.

"They're *all* vegan and gluten-free," the man answered. His tone was short and to the point. No-nonsense. Almost like he was irritated that they were in there.

How did one own a business but not like serving their customers? She wasn't sure, but it was at least working in her favor. She didn't appreciate rudeness in a guy, so she found the ability to look at him and not feel like she was in danger of dashing her life plans.

"Well, then. That makes this decision that much harder."

The guy gripped the edge of the counter and tucked his head toward his chest. Then pointed to the silver bell on the counter. "Ring that when you know what you want." With that, he spun around and pushed through the swinging door that led to the back.

With wide eyes, Hannah faced her cousin. "What was that about?"

"I have no idea," Brooke answered while she slowly shook her head. "He's always been nice to me. I'm not sure why he'd act like that."

For as attractive as that guy was, Hannah couldn't see past his attitude. Or how poorly it reflected upon a town she wanted to leave anyway. All of that worked for her.

But it didn't work for her stomach, which growled a second later.

"We can still go to Carrie Ann's," Brooke said, grinning and pointing across the street.

Reluctantly, Hannah twisted her head to face the old-timey diner. It probably didn't smell like salad, and she might not find something that was vegan *or* gluten-free. But she'd at least be away from the rude guy.

The sexy guy.

The guy who'd made her curious but had also ticked her off.

She needed none of that, so she readily agreed. "Carrie Ann's it is."

However, she couldn't help the look she tossed over her shoulder at the juice bar as she left. Something tugged at her. Something she couldn't name. Something she didn't quite like.

Something that made her change her schedule.

One week. That was all she'd give this place.

Then she'd go back to Vermont, back to her regular life.

The life she'd worked too hard for to throw off course now.

2

*L*uke Steiner's heart ached. Hard.

In the back of his juice shop, he removed his baseball cap and ran a hand through his hair. He thought about how long it was getting, how he'd need to make an appointment with Violet or Willow at the salon. That'd have to wait though. At least until after he took Ralph to his follow-up appointment.

The chocolate Lab he'd had since college wasn't doing well. Valley fever, likely picked up from a hike down in Phoenix. The vet had said they could try medicine to see if he'd get better, or...

He wasn't ready for that. Not even close. And neither was Ralph.

Nine years just wasn't enough with him.

He seemed to be doing better, but in twenty minutes, he'd find out if the medicine was working or not.

That didn't mean he'd needed to be such a jerk to the women out front. Especially Brooke. She'd been nothing but supportive since she'd come into town to build her sanctuary. The last thing she deserved was poor treatment from him. Same with the other woman.

The one Luke had only vaguely registered as being gorgeous. Health conscious, like him.

And gorgeous.

Oh, he'd thought that already.

He'd let that go the moment a thought of Ralph had entered his head. Treats he always bought his best pal were vegan and gluten-free, and that reminder had sent him into a tailspin.

Although he had to admit he'd been short-tempered from the second they'd walked in. But that was because he was so worried about his dog and their upcoming appointment.

The chances were fifty-fifty, the vet had said. But the medicine was worth a shot.

Luke thought *anything* was worth a shot to keep Ralph with him for as long as he could. His dog was a fighter, and Luke would fight with him.

He wouldn't have it any other way.

His dog was going to be fine and that was that.

He had to be.

In an effort not to scare off any more customers, he flipped the *open* sign to *closed* and locked the door behind him. It was near closing time anyway, and with the diner right across the street, he figured most people could just go there to get their salad if they really wanted one. He'd be back the next day to serve up fresh juice while Ralph was comfortable at home.

The vet was right across Soul Road, so he crossed the street, his heart pinching harder. He'd dropped Ralph off earlier to get checked out, and it was time to pick him up.

And find out the news.

"Hey, Sylvia," he said to the woman at the front desk.

"Luke!" she replied warmly, stacking papers on her desk. Her graying hair shimmered like tinsel in the overhead fluorescent lighting. "Ralph is all ready to go home. I'll let Dr. Stevens know you're here and she'll bring him out, okay? Just have a seat and sit tight."

Her warm smile should have settled the sour pit in his stomach a little, but it didn't. He was concerned for his dog.

Though, when Ralph bounded out of the back with Dr. Stevens straining to hold on to his leash, he wondered if he didn't need to be.

"Here he is!" the vet said. Then she chuckled. "He's very excited to see you, it seems."

"Probably just excited to get home." Luke took Ralph's leash and gave him a scratch on his head. "Aren't you, bud?"

Dr. Steven's tilted her head to the side. "Eh, I'd put more stock in your presence. I haven't seen him this happy since you dropped him off, so I'm sure it's more about you."

"Maybe," Luke said as Ralph leapt up, his front paws nearly reaching Luke's shoulders. He hadn't expected his dog to get so big, but at one hundred and ten pounds, Ralph was nearly as tall as Luke when he stood on his hind legs. "I'll go with that." Then he stroked his dog's back.

"Here's the refill on the meds," Dr. Stevens told him, reaching for a small paper bag Sylvia had placed on the counter. "Keep giving him one of these pills twice a day. If he won't take them on his own, use some peanut butter. Pups love peanut butter, don't they?" She winked at the dog.

That piqued Ralph's attention, and he sat as though he were going to get a spoonful right there in the office.

"When we get home, bud," Luke laughed. Then he bent and lowered his voice. "You can have all the peanut butter you want when we're at home."

That made Dr. Stevens laugh. "I wouldn't go that far."

Luke accepted the bag from the vet and gave her the saddest smile he could manage. "What are the odds now? Am I looking at months? Weeks? I need to be prepared." His voice broke on the last word as a knot formed in his throat. And his stomach.

"Well," she started, staring at Ralph. She filled her chest with a deep breath. "I think we caught it early enough, but let's see him here again in three weeks. We'll take more x-rays and send out another titer test, but today's results were positive. Just make sure you stay on track with the medicine, okay? I think Ralph is a trooper though. He'll make it through this." She patted the dog's head.

Relief bloomed in Luke's chest, but he didn't want to get his hopes up. He wouldn't quit on Ralph, though he wanted to be realistic. He was nothing if not a planner, someone who thought things through and made careful choices. At this point in his life, he couldn't afford not to be.

The first thing he'd do when he got home with his dog was make careful preparations to make sure he disbursed meds at the right time. Then he'd get Ralph comfy so he could rest and focus on getting better.

He could do this.

Everything would be fine.

"Thank you," he told the vet, some of that relief leaking into his voice. "I'm glad he has you."

Dr. Stevens put a hand on his shoulder. "And I'm glad Ralph has you. Another dog parent might not have noticed what you did so early."

He couldn't imagine that, but he was glad he'd caught it.

"Make that appointment with Sylvia and then get our patient home. We'll see you soon, okay, Ralph?"

Ralph barked his answer, and Dr. Stevens smiled as she waved goodbye. Once she was gone, Luke made Ralph's next appointment and then took him to his car across Soul Road, back by the juice shop. When he started his car, he noticed two familiar faces leaving Carrie Ann's Diner.

Brooke and the woman she'd brought into the juice shop earlier.

The women he'd been pretty rude to.

That was not the kind of man he was, and the last thing he needed was that on his conscience too while his dog was sick. He couldn't have that eating at him. As he drove Ralph home, Luke thought about how to make that better.

He landed on the idea to drive to the sanctuary and apologize. Maybe he'd even offer to help out as soon as Ralph wasn't sick anymore.

After dropping his dog off at home, he promised he'd be back as soon as possible. Then he got back into the car and headed toward Brooke's new animal sanctuary, located on the same property as Inn True Love, the local bed and breakfast. Penelope and Devon, the owners, had just expanded it with cabins out back, and he hadn't been there to see it since they'd started that in the spring. Now that it was late summer, he thought it was time.

It was also time to apologize to Brooke and her cousin.

When he pulled up in front of the tiny house Brooke had built on the property, he rehearsed what he'd say: that he was sorry he'd been rude, but his dog was sick and he'd been worried about bad news. He hoped that'd be enough to make them understand. Brooke knew him better than that too, so they'd get it. He was sure of it.

Except the look on Hannah's face when she opened the door made him think twice about that.

"You don't happen to have any salads with you, do you?" she asked, jumping right back into the snark from before.

"No, I don't. That's not why I'm here."

"Then I'm not sure why you're here." There was an edge to her voice, one he couldn't blame her for.

Taken aback, he raised his eyebrows. "I was about to explain why."

She stepped out of the doorway, which pushed him back a step. "I don't think it really matters unless you're here to offer up some help with this place."

"Actually, that's exactly why I am here," he told her. "I wanted to apologize for what happened at my shop earlier."

Her face softened a little, but only for a moment. He thought he'd imagined it when she spoke next. "Well, thanks. I had to resort to French fries for dinner so I didn't eat gluten. Luckily, they were air fried, but still." She started to go back inside, but for reasons unknown, he ended up stopping her.

"Carrie Ann's isn't the only place to eat around here. You could have found something else." The words had flown out of his mouth before he'd thought it through—which was so unlike him. But after the day he'd had...

Anything was possible.

"Uh, we tried," she reminded him. "We went to *your* place first."

He went to apologize for that again. He really was sorry. But she spoke up first.

"Either way, this town is the size of a penny. I have no clue why my cousin thinks this is a good idea, but Brooke's, well..." As she trailed off, Luke tried to fill in the blank. Kind? Compassionate? All things this cousin of hers didn't seem to be? "She's dedicated. When she gets an idea, she runs with it."

"Seems like an animal sanctuary is a good idea to me," he replied, thinking of his dog.

"Yeah, absolutely," the woman said, agreeing with him for the first time. "But here?"

Luke's blood pressure rose at that question. He loved this town, small though it was. "Why not here?"

The woman blinked several times as if the answer were obvious. "Have you been here long? Did the legend of this town actually happen to you? Is that why you like it so much?"

He rolled his eyes and pinched the bridge of his nose. He might have gone through this with her on any other day, but this day was like none other. All he wanted to do was make sure his dog was okay and sleep this whole frustrating nightmare off.

Still, he answered her with the truth. "No, it hasn't."

The legend of the town, that everyone found their true love in True Love, wasn't something he believed in. Maybe lots of folks had fallen in love there, but lots of folks fell in love in lots of places. It had nothing to do with their proximity to the town itself. Nothing to do with that at all.

At least, he hoped it didn't.

When he caught her gaze again, her face had that soft quality to it again. Like she'd felt the depth of his answer, not just the hollowness from the words he'd used.

Then she schooled it away. "What time can you be here tomorrow?"

"Tomorrow?" he asked, shocked. "I can't tomorrow. I was thinking maybe in a month or so."

Her eyes flashed wide. "A month? No. This week. It has to be this week," she insisted. "I have to get back home and to my job as soon as possible, so we need the help now."

If Brooke had been the one demanding this, he probably would have turned her down. Or kept negotiating. It wasn't like he didn't want to help out. He simply had too much going on, and she never would have spoken to him like this. But with the way this woman got on his nerves—and under his skin—he'd do what he could to make her wish come true.

"Fine," he told her. Then he spun away, and on his way back to his car, he said, "I'll be here at six."

The sooner she was gone, the sooner he could go back to his regular life.

The life where all he needed was his business and his dog, not a gorgeous woman who would skip town as soon as she could.

The life he'd worked too hard for to throw off course now.

3

"*I*'d love to help!" Misty, the owner of True Love Blooms, said to Hannah. "I actually got into floral arrangements through vegetable gardens. Those were my first love, so it'll be exciting to get back to that at Brooke's sanctuary."

"Great." Hannah crossed that off the list Brooke had given her after dinner.

After Juice Shop Guy had left.

After she'd berated herself for being rude back to him.

He'd gone there to apologize. He hadn't deserved that. But she'd been caught off guard, and French fries for dinner had made her moody. This whole trip had made her moody. She couldn't pinpoint why except that she felt like she was letting her clients down, but thinking that hard wasn't her strong suit.

She guessed she and Brooke were similar in that aspect.

They got ideas and ran with them.

That's how Hannah had ended up as a life coach. She'd gotten the itch to do it and that'd been that. Schooling and training later, she'd set up her website, made her list of services, and worked out prices with the people who'd emailed her. For the last two years, that's what she'd been doing.

But if she dug deep enough into her own life, she'd realize something wasn't right.

Maybe it stemmed from Jack and how he'd left her high and dry. Or maybe it stemmed from something else. She hadn't bothered to dig that deep for a reason and she wasn't starting now.

Instead, she was going to ask Misty for the next thing on the list. This one was for her though.

"Also," she said before lifting her gaze from her phone, "do you happen to know good places to hike around here? Trails or paths with good scenery, that kind of thing? My cousin wasn't very helpful with that."

Misty's lips curved into a soft frown. "You know, I really don't. This place keeps me pretty busy with it being wedding season and all." But then she snapped her fingers. "Oh! But I do know someone who might. Here." She pulled out a piece of paper, nabbed a pen from the holder by the register, and scribbled out ten digits. "This is Sylvia's phone number. Just text her and she'll tell you where to go."

"Thanks." Hannah stuffed the paper into the pocket of her jeans. "Give Brooke a call when you're ready to come by and plot out the garden. She'll be so excited to learn and grow her own food for the animals."

"And I'll be happy to help!" Misty smiled and waved as Hannah left the floral shop.

Stepping out onto the sidewalk, she felt an odd sense of peace wash over her. When she thought about it, she decided it'd come from checking something off her to-do list. Brooke would now have help with a vegetable garden for the sanctuary —that was something Hannah could be proud of. She'd done that. Of course she felt peace.

But that peace vanished the second she peeked across the street.

Main Squeeze was right on the other side, the sign gleaming in the late evening sun as though it were mocking her.

"Ugh," she said out loud. Inwardly, she complained about how small this town was.

Would she run into that guy or signs of him everywhere she went? She hoped he wasn't into hiking. As long as she could find a trail with some peace and quiet, a place with no signs of Luke or reminders of her past, she'd be fine for the week. Just the single week. Nothing more.

Otherwise, it'd be a long one.

A *really* long one.

It was her turn to apologize. She knew that. She shouldn't have been so short with him. While she didn't want to pull the "he started it first" card, she was feeling grumpy from all of the travel, the unhealthy dinner, and getting straight to work for her cousin. The sooner she got home, the sooner she could get back to her regular schedule. That's what she needed.

Not a distraction in the form of a sexy man with a penchant for rudeness.

Not a man who might derail her life the way Jack had.

Not a reason to stay in this teeny, tiny town.

Back in her car, she pulled her cell phone from her purse. Once she had the number Misty had given her in her hand, she created a new text message and typed one in.

HANNAH: Hi there, Sylvia. Misty gave me your number. I hope that's okay. I'm visiting True Love and looking for good trails and paths to hike. Any leads near the inn would be good. Thanks.

SHE HIT send and then started the car. As she drove back to the sanctuary, she hoped she'd get a message before she went to bed. It was already way past her usual bedtime on the East Coast, so she'd probably fall asleep as soon as her head hit the pillow. The rest of Brooke's to-do list would have to wait until the morning.

After her hike.

Daily exercise was a must for her. She did it out of necessity and habit more than a desire to be healthy. It was a means to feel her best and stay clearheaded for her clients. She'd get that hike in first thing. Then she'd be all Brooke's for the rest of the day.

No matter how much she was regretting the decision to go there now.

The drive back was quick, and she almost knew it by heart already. She supposed she could add that tiny thing to her pro column about this town: simple navigation.

But that was because they didn't have the plethora of options she was used to. No Target. No Whole Foods. No True Foods Kitchen—or even a Subway.

She hadn't thought she needed a lot before, but she knew now. None of those things felt like a lot. Living in a town like this, without those things? She couldn't picture herself doing that.

Not that it mattered. She had a home in Vermont to go back to. That's what she'd do when this week was up.

Inside the tiny house, she found her cousin reading on her tablet in the only chair in the "living room" area.

"You're back! What did Misty say?" Brooke asked, setting her tablet on the kitchen sink—without even getting up from her chair.

This was another thing Hannah didn't understand: the obsession with tiny homes. She couldn't imagine squeezing her entire life into one—that was for sure.

"She's happy to help," Hannah answered as she shut the

door. "Call her and let her know when you want her to come over."

A big smile curled Brooke's mouth. "I will. Thanks so much for doing that. I was able to get Stella into her barn for the night while you were gone."

"Aww, good."

"But I can't wait until the other animals get here! Three pigs are coming in two days, and Flagstaff had a group of five goats that need a home. They'll be here by the end of the week. We're going to fill up here soon!" Brooke clapped her hands, excitement pouring out of her.

While Hannah didn't share her extreme enthusiasm for this, she definitely liked seeing her cousin so happy. There'd been a time when neither of them had had much to look forward to, so it was nice to experience this hopeful, optimistic side of Brooke.

Hannah went to reply to Brooke's news, but her phone buzzed in her purse. She held up a finger as she reached into her bag, and when she removed her cell, an unknown number flashed on her screen.

"Everything okay?" Brooke asked.

"Oh, yeah. Probably just a text from Misty's friend."

Her cousin quirked an eyebrow. "A guy friend?"

At that, Hannah scoffed, though it came out like a sharp laugh. "Yeah right. It's actually someone named Sylvia. I guess she knows a lot about hiking in the area, so hopefully this is a suggestion about where to go in the morning."

Brooke nodded, the motion saying she didn't understand Hannah's enthusiasm for hiking. "All righty. Good luck with that." She got out of her chair and went to the door, just one and a half steps away. "While there's still a little light, I'm going to go dig another hole or two for the pig fencing. I'll try not to wake you when I come back."

Hannah shook her head. "Oh, you won't. I'll be out like a

light. Have fun though." She smirked and waved to Brooke, who headed back out into the summer evening.

That was Hannah's cue to open that text message. But what she found wasn't at all what she'd been expecting.

Unknown: Hello there, stranger. I'm not Sylvia, but you're in luck. I happen to know all about hiking in True Love.

Hannah: Oh, I'm sorry. I must have read the number wrong. Thank you though.

She fired that message off and then dug into her pocket for that number again. After checking every single digit, she realized it hadn't been her mistake after all. That was in fact the number Misty had given her. Why wasn't it the right one though?

And, more importantly, *who* was it?

She'd ask, but she'd already sent a text that felt final. In this instance, she'd tell her clients to leave well enough alone and move on. Not knowing everything was A-okay. Life wasn't about having all the answers—it was about having all the experiences. Like the things she'd experience in a small town called True Love before she went back home.

In that moment though, she wanted to experience sleep.

She got into her pajamas and then hiked up the ladder to the loft, where two twin beds lay next to each other with about six inches of space between them. Brooke had put fresh sheets on both that morning, and Hannah turned her side down before sliding into bed. Then she put her phone on the floor next to the bed and snuggled against her pillow.

Ahh, blessed sleep.

In three...two...

Her phone buzzed just before *one.*

She blinked her eyes open and reached for her phone.

Unknown: I'd like to help if you still want it. I can ask Sylvia myself, or I can just tell you my favorites. I think they're worth it, especially if you're only here a short time.

She wasn't sure what to say to that. It felt weird to text a stranger back and ask for help. While she thought it over though, another message came through.

Unknown: And I've had a rough day, so it'd be great if I could turn it around by sharing my little-known gems, the best-kept secrets of True Love's finest hikes. So...what do you say?

Some of Hannah's hardened exterior melted at that. This was more of what she'd expected from small-town living. Happy people helping each other out. Not the rude juice guy who couldn't be bothered to help his customers.

Even though he'd driven to the sanctuary to apologize.

Even though he was going to volunteer at the sanctuary to help get her back home sooner.

Even though he was *really* cute.

No. She didn't need any of that. It'd only derail her plan to keep herself focused on her work and getting back home. What she did need, however, was help finding a good trail. She focused on that instead and let the kind stranger on the other end of the text message help like they wanted to.

With a smile on her lips, she replied to that message.

Hannah: Actually, I'd really like that. Thank you.

4

When Luke's alarm went off at five forty the next morning, it was nothing new. Even though he didn't open his shop until eight most mornings, he loved getting up early in the summer and hitting the trails. Usually, he'd take Ralph, but he'd skipped a lot this summer since his dog had gotten stick.

This morning, however, he packed Ralph up into his car and headed out to the sanctuary. Some fresh air would do both of them some good.

He'd need all the fresh air he could get, too. Working side by side with the woman who'd all but begged him to volunteer there might kill him.

Hannah. Her name was Hannah.

And the morning sun shone on her long hair, creating a halo affect around her head as she worked out in the field.

That made him laugh. Halo, huh? She was anything but an angel—he was sure of that.

She'd been rude. Kind of cold. Though none of that negated how good she looked while she helped Brooke put up a fence. As she stacked lumber and took a break to pet a cow, he couldn't help but admire her strength—and the small kindness she was showing the animal.

Maybe she wasn't so bad after all.

Time would tell.

Ralph nudged him as if to say he should go find out. Luke didn't necessarily agree, but he *had* agreed to show up at six, and it was six on the nose.

"All right, bud. I guess we're doing this. Helping out so we can get her home. Come on." He opened the door and Ralph bounded out, not looking like the sick dog he'd been a couple of weeks ago.

Perhaps the medicine really was working and he needed to stop worrying.

He'd leave the worrying to other areas of his life, like how he was going to get along with this woman as he worked toward getting her the heck out of town.

"Hey, Luke!" Brooke waved at him as he approached.

He wasn't sure if it was the sound of her voice or his name on her lips that had Hannah whipping her head in his direction.

"What are you doing here?" she called out to him, her brow furrowed and her gloved hands on her hips.

Freezing in his tracks, he narrowed his eyes at her and tilted his head. "I said I'd be here at six, didn't I?"

Her head jerked backward. "I didn't think you meant six in the *morning.*"

"The shop is open at six p.m., so it'd have to be in the morning."

She mumbled something under her breath about working with him all day, but then she slipped her gloves off and headed toward the tiny house. "I need a water break."

Ralph followed after her, so he yelled for his dog to come back and the dog complied.

"Sorry about her," Brooke said. "I'm honestly not sure what's gotten into her. I thought maybe it was just her long trip here, but now, I don't know."

He shrugged, not wanting Brooke to feel like she had to figure her cousin out.

Then she wiped her forehead, already breaking a sweat this early in the day. "Did you sign up to volunteer? We'll actually need more help tomorrow when the pigs get here, but I'm sure I can find you something to do today. We're going to need help until...well, forever," she said, looking around and laughing lightly.

"I don't think I have forever in me, but I have a couple of days." He gestured toward Ralph. "As long as you don't mind me bringing him. I'm working most of the day as it is. This could be good for him to stretch and be outside."

Brooke gave him a *duh* expression. "This is an animal sanctuary, Luke. Of course your dog is welcome here." She smiled at him and waved him over to where she'd been working.

While he followed her, his phone pinged in his pocket. He wondered if it was the vet with more news, though that was basically impossible. Still, he decided to check it just in case. However, it wasn't the vet.

Unknown: Hey, stranger. Thanks for that trail recommendation yesterday. I went out there this morning and really enjoyed it.

Ahh, yes. The person who'd thought he was Sylvia. At least he'd been able to help. Doing that had turned his day around, and it made him smile as he tapped out his reply.

Luke: I'm glad I could be of service. If you need anything else while you're here, just let me know.

Unknown: Thanks. I'll probably be busy, but my morning hikes will keep me sane. I owe that to you.

That smile grew as he slid his phone back into his pocket of his jeans. If something good could happen because of a wrong number, he'd take it. He needed to focus on something positive while things were chaotic around him.

While he listened to Brooke's to-do list for the day, he put on the gloves he'd brought. It seemed like a lot of tasks, but he'd do what he could in the hour and a half he could give her. Then he'd need to take a quick shower at home and open his shop.

And he'd feel like he'd accomplished his goal of helping Hannah go back home.

Hannah, who came out of the house looking focused and ready to report for duty.

He couldn't help it. He liked that about her. He didn't want to, but it'd help the cause, so it worked.

"Ready to get this show on the road?" he asked to help lighten the mood.

"Yep," she said, nodding once in a sharp movement. "Let's do this."

He started to follow her, thinking they'd work together, although that sounded like a disaster waiting to happen.

Hannah must have thought that too, because she spun to face him and then pointed to the barn. "Can you work on painting this morning?"

Lifting his gloved hands, he said, "But don't you want my muscle for building that fence?"

She peeked over her shoulder and then firmed up her stance. "No, I think we can handle it, but thanks."

"Are you sure? Because I could be useful there. Save you some of that fiery energy you've already built up so early in the morning." He smirked at her, hoping it'd break the ice.

But it didn't. "And I can use that fiery energy on building the fence with Brooke. The barn needs a fresh coat of paint though. Stella will appreciate it."

"Stella?" he asked, raising his eyebrows.

She jutted her chin toward the barn. "Stella. The cow."

The way she'd said it made him wonder if she really meant that or she was being sarcastic. Perhaps she didn't share her cousin's love of animals. And that didn't sit well with Luke. He didn't have aspirations of owning a sanctuary like Brooke did, but he couldn't imagine someone not loving animals. Or at least liking them. He'd seen her with the cow though. It hadn't seemed like she had any disdain for the animal.

Those thoughts faded the moment Ralph ran up between him and Hannah and her eyes lit up.

"Oh, hey there," she said, reaching a hand out to him. Then she flicked her gaze up to Luke. "Is this one yours?"

Proudly, he nodded. "Yep," he replied, patting the dog on his back. "This is Ralph."

She started to crouch closer to Ralph, who gave her his paw, which made her stay upright. When she accepted his paw, he rose to his full height and licked the side of her face. Then an honest-to-God giggle flew out of her mouth.

"Oh my gosh!" she exclaimed, her eyes squeezed shut. The happiest expression took her face over.

It was the first time Luke had seen her that way, and it entranced him in a way he hadn't expected.

A happy Hannah was, in a word, beautiful.

He almost couldn't believe it.

He had to believe his eyes though. And that his dog hadn't meant to push her over in his excitement, but that's exactly what he'd done.

Shaking out of his Hannah-induced stupor, he rushed over to her. With her arms flailing, he hoped to catch her before she fell. And when he did, the only thing more surprising than how beautiful she was while laughing was how good she felt in his arms.

Way.

Too.

Good.

So good that he couldn't let her go right away.

For some reason, she didn't look like she wanted him to, either.

They stayed like that for several seconds, though to Luke, it felt like an eternity. Somehow, that was fine by him. Something felt so right about holding her.

Until she snapped out of their trance, righted herself, and cleared her throat. She glanced all around, at everything but him, as she said, "Okay, then. I'm going to go work on the fence. Over there. By myself."

Sooner than he could reply, she took off in that direction.

That left him chuckling to himself. Maybe this woman had a good side to her after all. He warned himself not to worry about it, not to get attached. It was clear she wanted to go back home, wherever that was. And he had his business to run and a dog to take care of.

In the meantime, he'd paint the barn as much as he could until he had to head out.

However, a peek over his shoulder let him know that she was doing the same. Their gazes met, and she quickly spun her head back around after getting caught. He hadn't missed the curve of her lips though, the way they'd tipped up toward the sun before she'd forced them flat.

She intrigued him. He'd give her that.

And she liked his dog. That was *definitely* a plus.

Maybe they needed to start over. Fresh. With a clean slate.

Or maybe he needed to remember that she was leaving and this wasn't a good idea. He needed to take care of his dog, run his shop, and not let another woman throw his life off course.

No, he wouldn't let that happen again.

5

"Uh, what was *that* about?" Brooke asked the moment Hannah returned to work on the pig fences.

Hannah pretended not to know what she was talking about. "What was what about?"

With a finger pointed in Luke's direction, Brooke said, "That."

"Nothing," Hannah replied quickly. Too quickly. Then she pushed Brooke's finger out of the air before Luke caught them talking about him.

Brooke laughed as she hammered a post into the dirt. "Nothing. Okay. Whatever you say."

"What?" Hannah helped her cousin make sure the next one was lined up. "The barn needs to be painted. Why can't he work on that while we do this?"

With wide eyes that screamed *Isn't it obvious?* Brooke said, "Because he could have helped put this fence in. Painting the barn is much easier than this." Then she shrugged and made a face. "Plus, I know you've seen those muscles."

Caught, Hannah bristled. "Okay, but he's been kind of rude, Brooke."

"Which is unusual for him. I've been to his shop a few times and he's been nothing but nice to me."

"Well, he's not right now, so he can stay over there."

"Maybe something's wrong though. He seems stressed out, like he's worried about something."

Hannah eyed her cousin suspiciously. "Is that the feeling you get?"

Brooke nodded and peeked over at Luke.

"We don't need that energy over here, do we?" Hannah asked, doing everything she could not to also look at him. "We have a lot of work to do."

Brooke let the next post fall to the grass as she stood up straight and dusted her gloved hands. "I suppose, but that would mean you should go over to the bad energy side of this place and help him paint the barn."

"Me?" Hannah asked, incredulous. She jabbed a finger into her chest for good measure. "Why me? I'm just stressed out too."

"And it'd be rude of me to point out that you're reacting the same way he is, but..." Brooke trailed off, and when Hannah looked at her, she winked. Then she hammered the next post in.

All while Hannah did what she'd told herself she shouldn't do.

She glanced back at Luke, but the glance turned into a lingering stare while she watched him get the paint and brushes ready to put a fresh coat on the barn. Ralph sprinted back and forth between Stella and Luke, running around like a happy dog. It seemed like Luke could barely take his eyes off the dog, and that warmed Hannah's heart. The way he smiled as he watched the pup gave her the feeling that he wasn't a totally bad guy.

Plus, she had to admit that being in his arms had already convinced her of that.

No one had ever caught her like that.

No one had ever saved her from falling.

No one had ever held her that way.

She wouldn't forget that any time soon, though it didn't take away all of the other memories she had of this man. The ones where he hadn't been so nice.

And the ones where *she* hadn't been kind, either.

Part of her wondered if they'd simply gotten off on the wrong foot. Maybe they were both stressed about something and they'd let it come out in the wrong way.

But another part of her realized that none of it would matter once she was back on a plane to Vermont.

———

LATER THAT NIGHT, exhausted from finishing up the pig pens, Hannah settled in front of her laptop. Brooke had gone out to pick up groceries, but Hannah hadn't wanted to chance running into Luke. Not when she was so conflicted about him.

She pulled her email up, expecting a whole bunch of them. She'd never left her clients this long before. It'd only been two days, but as a life coach, she wanted to be available all the time. Life happened all the time, so she should be there.

All she found, however, were two emails. One of them was spam. She opened the one that wasn't, her heart speeding up in anticipation.

From: lucy.harden1@email.com

To: hannah@hannahlockhartcoach.com

Subject: Coaching

Hey, Hannah! I hope your vacation is going well. I hope it's okay that I'm reaching out while you're gone, but I'm having an issue. Think we can schedule a time to work on it? Thanks!

Hannah hit the reply button as quickly as she could. The

email had come in *yesterday*, and the panic whipping throughout her body made the words race from her fingers.

From: hannah@hannahlockhartcoach.com
To: lucy.harden1@email.com
Subject: Re: Coaching

Of course, Lucy! I'd be happy to. Pick a time and we'll set up a web call. So sorry it's taken me this long to get back to you, but I look forward to our coaching session.

Hannah Lockhart
Personal Life Coach / Business Goal-Getter

When she checked the time, she realized that Lucy was likely in bed already. Her New York powerhouse client sometimes needed a push in the right direction. That go-get-em attitude wore Lucy out to the point where she froze during decision-making, so Hannah had worked with her on a few things.

One, she could count to five and then *bam*. She had to choose one way or the other and trust that it was right.

Or, two, she could make a pro/con list and decide that way.

So far, Lucy had been doing well with both of these strategies. Every now and then, though, she needed some reassurance. That was what Hannah loved about her job: being there for her clients in the hard times. Even though the whole point of her job was to make sure they didn't need her again, she didn't mind. Getting them to that point was the goal.

Lucy was almost there. If Hannah were Brooke, she'd be able to "feel" it.

She didn't get those "feelings" Brooke usually got though. They'd probably help her out, but she relied on actions. Not how she felt.

Actions, not feelings, had gotten her to where she was now. Actions, not feelings, had built her business and given her her freedom. Actions, not feelings, had made her the woman she'd become.

Feelings had gotten her into trouble.

Pushing all of that aside, she shut her laptop down and snagged her phone off the kitchen sink. She'd put it there because, well, there was nowhere else to put it. The small table Brooke had set up in front of the sitting space had only enough room for her computer. After rising from the chair, she took her phone outside, the cramped space getting to her.

In the setting sun, she stretched her legs. She'd been worried that the elevation would bother her. At nearly seven thousand feet, True Love beat her home's elevation by a mile. So far though, the fresh air had done her some good. Even on her hikes, she hadn't been troubled by being up so high in the mountains.

Speaking of hikes...

Which one would she do tomorrow?

After checking to see if Lucy had emailed her, she pulled up her text messages and found the thread with her helpful stranger. The person had recommended a couple of them, but she wondered if other hidden gems could be found while she was in town. She had no idea when she'd return to the town, so she wanted to pack it all in now.

Hannah: I'm going to check out another trail tomorrow. I have a few more days to check out more, so if you have other suggestions, I'd be open to hearing them.

It was already nine p.m. She didn't know the stranger's schedule, but even she should have been up in the loft, getting ready for bed. After taking a few more deep breaths of fresh mountain air, she scooped her phone up and started to head inside.

But her phone buzzed in her hand before she'd even opened the door.

Unknown: Actually, I have a bunch. Though this town is small, we have a lot to offer. Hikes included.

Another text followed with a list of trails. At least eight of them.

She appreciated that she'd messaged the wrong number but received help anyway. That was definitely a mark in the pro column. Helpful strangers. What a concept.

Hannah: Thank you. You've been so very helpful. If I can do anything to return the favor, please let me know.

This time, she expected to receive some kind of generic response. A *thanks, but that's okay* kind of deal. Maybe they'd say that helping her was enough for them. That seemed like the kind of thing a nice person from True Love would say.

Not a person like Luke, even if Brooke insisted he wasn't normally like that.

She scoffed at herself for thinking about him yet again. What she needed was to meet more people in town so the one person she did know didn't always pop up in her mind. Or she just needed to get back home like she planned to do.

But when her phone went off again, that's not the type of message she received.

Unknown: Actually... Can I take you up on that right now? I have a burning question I need an answer to. It's kind of serious, and only you can help.

That surprised her. She didn't know this person, but they trusted her for something like this? Good thing life coaching was her specialty. Maybe the rest of her clients didn't need her, but the person on the other end of this message did, and that made her feel good.

Hannah: Yeah, sure. What's up?

With her eyes glued to her phone for an incoming message, she made her way inside. At the ladder to the loft, the screen brightened with their response.

And the question they'd posed made her burst into much-needed laughter.

Unknown: Are you one of those weird people who thinks pineapple goes on pizza?

6

*U*nknown: That assumes I actually like pizza.

Unknown: But no, don't worry. I'm not one of *them.*

As Luke grabbed his toothbrush, he laughed out loud at that response. He wasn't even sure why he'd asked, but after a long day of painting, juicing, and walking Ralph, he'd needed a moment of levity. Humor. Lightheartedness. Something fun.

Pizza was always a fun topic.

Sure, he ran a juice shop, but who didn't like pizza?

Which brought him back to the message with this stranger.

Luke: Good answer. But uh, everyone likes pizza. It's an unwritten law.

Unknown: I'd disagree, but maybe that's an unwritten law in True Love and I just haven't been here long enough yet.

Luke: That could be it. I can help you brush up on all the True Love unwritten laws, like everyone loves pizza, no one complains about the weather, and you have to eat at Carrie Ann's at least once a week or you're not a real resident.

He wanted to say something about his juice bar, but he also

liked being anonymous. The appeal of it made this fun, and he needed some fun.

Brushing his teeth wasn't exactly fun, but the anticipation of receiving another text from this stranger was.

Unknown: Does that mean I have to go to Carrie Ann's, eat pizza, and talk about how awesome Arizona temperatures are at least once while I'm here?

Luke almost choked on toothpaste as he read that message. Laughing, he spit it out, rinsed his toothbrush, and headed to bed. With a knee against his mattress, he let his fingers fly over his phone's keyboard.

Luke: Actually, Carrie Ann's doesn't have pizza. I'm not sure how the town committee hasn't noticed that, but I'll be sure to bring it up. See? You're already contributing.

Unknown: Well, I'm only here for a few more days. Maybe another week or so. I'll do what I can while I'm still here though.

Luke slid under his covers and wondered how to respond to that. It wasn't like he knew this person, but he didn't like the idea of them leaving. So many tourists flew in and out of the area, so he was used to it. Still, he'd never connected with any of them.

Not that he'd connected with this person. Whoever it was.

That made more questions swirl in his head.

Luke: Just a quick trip here? Visiting family?

Unknown: Yep. Gotta love relatives who live in such scenic areas, with great hiking trails to choose from. Even if they know nothing about them and you have to text a stranger on accident to find out which ones are good.

Luke: You do have to love that, huh. Thank goodness for strangers. ;) Have fun on the trail tomorrow.

He set his phone on his nightstand, thinking he needed to leave well enough alone. None of the questions about who this stranger was or what they were doing in True Love mattered in the end. But when his cell chimed with another text, he thought maybe those things did matter.

Unknown: Thanks. Maybe I'll see you out there. I'll be the woman falling asleep on the trail because it's been hard to get used to this time zone. Why doesn't Arizona do Daylight Savings?

Luke: I don't know, but I'll be the guy who put a pillow at the end of the trail for you.

Unknown: So sweet of you. Goodnight.

Luke: Sleep tight.

He set his phone back on the nightstand facedown this time. They'd said their goodbyes, so he could go to sleep now. However, the buzzing in his veins made him want to do anything but rest. But with Ralph curled up at the end of the bed, he closed his eyes and let the stress of everything drain away.

His stranger was a woman.

A kind, thoughtful, funny woman.

A woman he looked forward to talking to some more.

Even though it probably wouldn't go anywhere.

And, based on his past, it *shouldn't* go anywhere.

AT THE SANCTUARY the next morning, Luke let Ralph out of his car. The dog took off at a sprint, running over to Stella, his friend from yesterday. He wasn't sure how he'd break it to the poor guy that it'd never work between them, but he'd let Ralph figure it out on his own.

Or maybe Stella would let him down gently.

Unlike how things were going with him and Hannah.

Not that it'd ever been in question. He'd ruined it from the start, and then she'd proven that she wasn't the one for him anyway. She had her foot out the door already, and she didn't seem to like being around him. Even though he'd caught her staring the day before, he didn't think too much about it.

He'd even pushed aside that memory of her in his arms. It'd been tough but for the best.

But on this particular morning, Hannah didn't seem so bristly.

With her long hair pulled up into a ponytail, he could see the slope of her neck. As she tilted her head back and forth to stretch it, her hair swayed back and forth. It brushed against the back of her tank top, which looked like the kind women wore for exercise. Even Brooke was dressed in workout clothes as they walked toward him from the tree line.

"Hey," Brooke said, waving. "Back again?"

He glanced at the barn. "I still have some painting to do. Can't leave you ladies to finish up my job."

Hannah ran the back of her arm across her forehead. "Thanks. That'd be helpful."

Well, color him impressed. "Really? No snide remark about how I might do it wrong?"

She shook her head, the hint of a smile ghosting over her lips. "Not today. I got my exercise in, and Brooke bought some healthy groceries, so I feel better today."

"Ahh," he replied. "So the impatience and eagerness to get away from me yesterday. All of that. It wasn't about me?" He was teasing, but her answer surprised him.

"Was yours about me?"

He peeked over at Ralph and thought about his business. Then he shook his head. "No."

"Okay, then." She flashed a tight smile and then waved her cousin on as she walked away. "Let's get to work, shall we?"

"What are you going to work on?" he called after her. He hadn't been able to help it. Seeing her this way was...refreshing. Interesting. Intriguing.

She spun to face him and then gestured with her head toward the back field. "Goat pens."

"Need help?" he shouted.

"Nope," she called back around a laugh.

A *laugh*.

A genuine laugh.

It made questions pop into his head before he could squash them.

What had gotten into her?

She was actually capable of laughter?

And why did he like it so much?

Two hours later, only half of the barn was painted. At this rate, he wouldn't be done until Friday, but he had to open the juice bar on Friday, so he couldn't make it to the sanctuary that morning. He'd let Brooke know the next morning. She and Hannah had taken off with the trailer to go pick up three pigs who'd get to live their lives at the sanctuary. He would have offered to go with, but he really needed to focus on his business.

The one he'd do anything to keep.

"Hey," Mateo said when Luke entered the juice bar. "How's it going over at the sanctuary?"

Luke stepped behind the counter and braced a hand on the edge. "It's good. I was hoping to get the barn fully painted this week, but hopefully they're okay with it being partly done."

"Need some help over there? I can see who I can round up."

Huh. That wasn't a bad idea. If Hannah wanted to leave this town as soon as possible, then maybe he should take Mateo up on that.

Though the voice was miniscule, he heard the voice that told him not to. It reasoned that Hannah would stay longer if the job didn't get finished right away. That small part of him wanted to hear that genuine laugh again, even if that idea was ridiculous.

"Maybe," is all he said.

"All right. Well, I got all the salads prepped and all but two of the dressings made. Now that you're here, I'll go get those other two done."

"No, that's okay." Luke passed his employee on the way to the back. "I got it, but thank you. You mind staying up here and manning the register?"

"You got it, boss." Mateo gave him a fake salute, which made them both crack grins. "Let me know if you need anything before I go at ten."

"Will do," Luke answered before pushing through the swinging door.

He wouldn't need anything else. Mateo worked hard enough for Luke's dream, so he'd let the kid head off to his summer college class at NAU to work toward his own dream. Luke was sure Mateo knew he wouldn't ask for any more help, seeing as he'd worked there for almost a year with him. It was kind of him to ask anyway. That's the kind of guy Mateo was.

For now, Luke would settle into his happy place: in front of his Vitamix with all of the ingredients he needed to make his vegan and gluten-free ranch dressing.

The moment he popped the first garlic clove into the blender, his phone chirped in his pocket. After taking his gloves off, he dug it out and found a new text.

From his mystery woman, which is how he'd saved her number in his phone.

Mystery Woman: It's a good thing there wasn't a pillow at the end of the trail this morning. I didn't actually need it after all.

Luke: Sorry. Someone kept me up too late last night with all of her incessant texting. Glad it worked out anyway though.

Mystery Woman: It did. I'm looking forward to trying out yet another trail tomorrow. But first, more family time.

Before he could respond to that, another text came through.

Mystery Woman: What about you? What are you up to today?

He wondered how specific to get. He still liked the anonymous thing, but he also liked their fun banter. Wanting that to continue, he tapped out a reply.

Luke: Oh, the usual. Volunteering, working my own business, taking my dog to the dog park, helping damsels in distress with sleeping accoutrements on their hikes. Ya know. That kind of thing.

He laughed to himself over how ridiculous this was. But he liked it. Almost as much as he liked making the food he sold at his juice bar. The next text made him laugh even harder.

Mystery Woman: Wow. What a knight in shining armor. I'm sure all of those damsels in distress thank you for your generosity. So humble you are. *wink*

Mystery Woman: Have a good day, sir.

Luke set his phone down, a big grin spreading all over his face. It only widened as he added cashews, dill, and water to the blender.

"What's that about?" Mateo said when he came into the back.

Luke answered without looking at him. "What's what?" But when Mateo stayed silent, he finally gave him his gaze.

"That." His employee pointed to Luke's face. "You don't normally look like that."

Trying to pass it off, Luke said, "You mean I don't smile ever?"

"Oh sure." Mateo stacked cucumbers in his arms to take to the front. "Just not like *that*." Then he pushed through the swinging door without elaborating.

Luke didn't want to think about it too hard. However, when he taste-tested that batch of ranch, he thought it'd never tasted better.

And he was forced to silently thank his mystery texter for his good mood. He typed a new text out to tell her just that.

Luke: Oh, I already am.

7

*O*n their way back with the pigs, Hannah clutched her phone. She squeezed it as though she could will another text from the mysterious guy on the other end. That wasn't how it worked though, and it was her turn anyway.

He was having a good day.

She hoped she had something to do with that.

When her phone vibrated in her fingers, she snapped it up to her face, her heart thudding a little harder in her chest. Maybe she *had* willed another message from him by sheer hope alone.

"Who's that?" Brooke asked from the driver's seat of the van.

Hannah pulled up the notification, but her heart slowed to its normal rhythm when she saw what it was. "Just spam email," she said, the adrenaline flowing from her body.

"Oh. Seemed like something important."

After deleting the email, she tucked her phone into her purse. If Brooke was noticing, she had to put the brakes on it. "Nope."

"You sure?" Brooke made a left turn into the lot for the sanctuary. "You looked pretty eager to see what it was."

Hannah shook her head. "I'm sure."

"Because earlier, you looked the same way at your phone."

Shrugging, she said, "Must have been a client." She barely got the words out over her nervousness.

"You look that way when *all* of your clients email you?" The curious smile on Brooke's mouth almost had Hannah cracking and telling the truth.

But she didn't want Brooke to have something to hold over her head. Something that might help Brooke convince her to stay in True Love after all.

As soon as the van was in park, Hannah hopped out of the car. "Let's just get the pigs to their home, okay?"

Brooke froze, her hands on the key in the ignition and her smile turning happy. "Home. I like that." Then she too got out of the vehicle and met Hannah around back.

It took almost twenty minutes to get the scared pigs out of the trailer one by one, but they finally did it. They'd tested the fence earlier to make sure there were no weak spots. They weren't two-hundred-pound pigs though. Time would tell if they'd hold up.

"Welcome home, you three!" Brooke excitedly clutched her hands together and crouched to their level. "I'm so glad you're here. And Stella is going to be so happy to have friends here on a regular basis. Luke's dog isn't enough around here."

The mention of Luke got Hannah's blood pressure to go up. Had they come to a truce earlier? Or were they merely avoiding each other to keep the peace? Honestly, she wasn't sure either way. All she knew for sure was that just his name piqued her interest. The man, with his backwards baseball cap and cargo shorts, did something to her—and nothing good could come of that.

The text message guy though...

That should have been more concerning. But it was fun, and she'd earned a little fun on her working vacation.

Luke was not fun.

He ran hot and cold.

And he was cute. Handsome. Sexy, even.

But not fun. Not really. Not the kind Hannah wanted to have.

What kind *did* she want to have? Had she even thought about it? No, not really, she supposed. But she knew deep down that Text Message Guy was the kind of fun she liked. Luke's unpredictable attitude? No, thanks.

Luckily, she didn't have to acknowledge any of that to Brooke. A man who appeared to be in his late thirties or early forties was approaching them from the inn's lobby. He came down the path from the back door, his hands in his pockets.

"Brooke? Who's this?" Hannah asked, motioning her head toward the guy.

When Brooke rose to her full height, she shielded her eyes from the sun. "Oh, that's Kyle, I think. He owns the ice cream shop in town—Gimme The Scoop."

"You think?"

"Yeah." Brooke started walking his way. "I'm still new here, remember?"

Hannah trailed behind her, accepting that answer. When the three of them converged though, that answer didn't seem all that acceptable any longer.

Maybe she didn't get her cousin's "feelings" about things, but there was no doubt what she was seeing between these two.

From the way Brooke blushed when she shook Kyle's hand to the way Kyle seemed hesitant to let go, Hannah knew exactly what the future held for them.

But she'd keep that ace in her back pocket for later too.

"Hi," Brooke said. "It's nice to see you again."

"Right." Kyle put his hand back into his pocket and rocked onto his heels. "We briefly met at the diner one time. A few weeks ago."

Brooke nodded, but that pink in her cheeks didn't go away. And it wasn't from the sun. "Yeah, exactly. You remember."

"Of course," Kyle answered.

And then they both went quiet as sparks flew and they held each other's gazes.

Oh, Hannah was *so* excited to pull this out when she needed to.

True love in True Love was happening right in front of her eyes. How much better did it get than that?

Did that mean the lore of the town was true? Hannah didn't know how long Kyle had lived there, but Brooke hadn't been there that long. That didn't bode well for Hannah, so she was glad she'd decided to stay for only a week. Her life did not need a complication like love. Not in a small town in Arizona.

Though a tiny tickle in the back of her brain nudged her in the opposite direction.

If that was about Luke, her brain could take a hike.

But maybe it was about Text Message Guy? He lived in town, and he was kind and caring. Much different from Jack. So maybe that wasn't a bad thing.

She cleared her throat to get rid of those thoughts, which jarred Kyle and Brooke from their love trance.

"What are you doing here?" Brooke asked him.

Kyle tossed his thumb and a glance over his shoulder. "Just brought the ice cream delivery to the inn. I do that once a week, and today's the day." Then he peeked behind Brooke. "Oh, wow. I haven't been back here yet, but it looks great. Who are those little guys?"

"The pigs!" Brooke's enthusiasm poured out of her. "We just

got them home, literally right now. I'll probably stay out here tonight to make sure they settle down."

"Ooh," Hannah interjected as she took the spot on the other side of her cousin. "Does that mean I get the entire tiny loft to myself tonight?"

"Ha ha," Brooke said, feigning laughter. "Yes, it does."

Kyle stood next to Brooke and looked over the pig pen. "That's a good idea, actually. Let them get used to this place and you so they're not figuring it out alone. It'll keep them from feeling too anxious."

"That's what I thought," Brooke breathily replied. Then she tilted her head at the man. "How do you know all of that?"

When Kyle didn't answer right away, Hannah leaned forward to see his face. A mask shrouded it, as if he were trying to push a memory down and forget the past.

"Just part of another life," he answered cryptically.

Hannah didn't need Brooke's "feelings" to understand. Her logic suited her well. So did her life coach training. She'd been taught what to look for and work with, so she knew that this man had been through something awful in that other life of his. It made her heart clench.

It also made her think that something between him and Brooke would be a really good thing. But she'd keep *that* in her back pocket until the time was right too.

"If you ever want to talk about it," Brooke told him, resting a gentle hand on his arm, "I'm always here. Literally." She smiled at him.

All at once, that mask fell away and a grateful grin tipped his lips up. "Thanks. I may take you up on that."

Hannah's heart released and her whole body warmed as she watched the two of them. She didn't want to believe it, but the proof was right in front of her eyes.

Maybe, just maybe, there was something special about this town.

And maybe, just maybe, she wondered if it could happen to her too.

8

*M*ystery Woman: Hey. Are you up?

Luke: I'm here. Thinking about me? *wink*

Mystery Woman: Actually… Is it weird if I say yes?

Luke's heart skipped a beat. He didn't want to own up to that, but he'd felt the absence of that beat down to his toes. Was she really thinking about him? He'd certainly done a lot of thinking about her all day. Curiosity was getting to him.

Who was she? Would he know when she went back home? Would they stop texting then? He wasn't sure why they were still texting, but he liked it. That much he was sure of.

Before he could reply, another message came through.

Mystery Woman: I mean, you messaged me back, so obviously I was thinking about you. *wink back*

At that, he laughed out loud. Then he called for Ralph, who lumbered up the stairs behind him. Was he getting slower? Was this a sign that the medicine wasn't working? Could it be possible that Ralph wasn't healing like Dr. Stevens thought?

This time when Luke's heart stopped beating for a moment, it had nothing to do with the mystery woman and everything to do with fear.

On the middle stair, the dog sprang to life, which flooded Luke with relief. Ralph took off for his usual spot on the bed, while Luke went into the bathroom to get ready for sleep. When he was done, he patted Ralph on his head.

"You scared me, bud." He pulled the covers back, and the mattress dipped with his weight as he climbed in. "But you're still fighting, aren't you?"

Ralph adjusted his head against his curled-up body and let out a long sigh.

"That's what I thought." Luke smiled at the dog and then fluffed his pillow, ready to let sleep take him under after that adrenaline rush of panic for his pup.

But he caught sight of his phone on his nightstand and remembered that his mystery woman had texted him. That made his heart flutter back to life. And when he picked his phone up, he saw another message in his notifications.

Mystery Woman: You still there? Did I scare you away? Or did you fall asleep on me already? Come on now. Even I'm still awake. Maybe I'm getting used to this time zone after all.

Luke wanted this woman to get more than used to this time zone. He wanted her to stay in it so they could continue getting to know each other. But texts could happen from anywhere, so maybe she'd continue to message him even after she went back home.

Though he'd wanted to say something playful back, a part of him wanted to share his worry with another person. He hadn't made too many friends while focusing on his business the last couple of years. Even though he was a member of this town, he hadn't felt fully settled there. Not like he'd felt in Tucson. Getting too close to his fellow townspeople had gotten him into hot water though.

Well, just one of the townspeople in particular.

That could happen again. Or he could make a friend who

wouldn't end up distracting him so much that he let his business go under. Maybe her not living in True Love would be the best thing for him after all.

He decided to get personal instead.

Luke: Yeah, here, sorry. Actually, my dog is sick. Getting better, but I thought for a moment that maybe the medicine wasn't working anymore.

His heart thudded as he waited for her response. They hadn't talked about things like this before, so he wasn't sure what she was going to say. The message that came in though... It didn't disappoint.

Mystery Woman: Oh my gosh, I'm so sorry to hear that. Dogs are literally the greatest thing on earth. I hope yours gets better soon. <3

Luke: Thank you for that. I don't have anyone here but the vet to share that with, and she's reassuring but not someone I should call in the middle of the night, you know? That's not really the relationship we have.

Knowing she was a dog lover only made this better. She understood, and she hadn't judged him. She'd been supportive. That counted for something. A lot.

Mystery Woman: Haha, no, probably not. It's best if you let her take care of just your dog, not you too.

Chuckling, Luke hit the reply button. He liked her sense of humor as well.

Ralph, it seemed, didn't like the disturbance of Luke's laughter though. When the bed shook a little, the dog peeked his head up, gave Luke a look, and sighed again.

Luke gave him a few strokes on his back. "Come on. You understand, don't you? Whatever you have going on with Stella, it's the same thing."

Except that it wasn't, he realized. Ralph got to see Stella in person. He knew who she was, even if it'd never work out. Two different species was almost equal to two different time zones, so maybe it *was* a little similar.

He started to type his next message, but another one from her came in first.

Mystery Woman: But hey, you have me now, right? I'm happy to listen to midnight blubbering about man's best friend in any time zone. Spare your vet the trouble, will you?

Luke: I'm touched. Really. How did this wrong number situation turn into *you* helping *me*?

That was the truth. She'd reached out to Sylvia, who'd turned out to be him. She'd wanted suggestions for hikes. And he'd offered to help out because that's what people did in this town. It's why he'd grown to love it so much, even if he hadn't truly immersed himself into it.

Now, she'd offered to be there for him. He really liked the sound of that.

Three little dots appeared on his screen. She was typing back. But then they disappeared. Then reappeared. Then vanished again.

Luke: Taking it back already? I can handle it. Just rip the Band-Aid off.

Mystery Woman: No, no. Of course not. What kind of friend would I be otherwise?

Luke: Friends, huh?

Mystery Woman: Yeah, I'd say so. Text friends. And your first order of text friend duty is to tell me if the grocery store in town has a good price on spinach. But if that's too much to ask from a text friend, just say the word and I'll rescind your title.

Luke laughed out loud again, though it didn't seem to disturb Ralph this time. Perhaps they both were getting used to these late-night chats before bed.

Luke: It depends. Are you making a salad? Doing some kind of weird art project with it? What's the purpose of this spinach?

Mystery Woman: First of all, don't judge me if I want to make spinach art, okay? Maybe that's a thing I do. You don't know.

Luke: You're absolutely right. Please accept my apology, and let the record show that we had our first text friend fight, which ended with me saying I'm sorry and getting in line to be the first to buy your weird spinach art.

Mystery Woman: Thank you. Apology accepted. Maybe for that, I'll sell it to you at a discount.

Luke: You are too kind to me. Too kind.

Mystery Woman: Actually, I just want to make a smoothie, but it seems the cousin I'm staying with does not have a blender, so forget the spinach. Carrie Ann's doesn't have smoothies, do they?

At that, he gulped. Did he dare name his shop and tell her to come in? If he did, he'd wonder if any of the women who showed up were her. His mystery woman. He wasn't sure he wanted to chance that, but he wasn't about to turn down business.

Luke: What about Main Squeeze? The name is a little hokey, but I've heard they have good smoothies. And they're right across the street from the diner, so it kind of counts as your weekly visit quota.

Those three dots showed up again. Blinking. Making him sweat. Would she take him up on that offer? Might he meet his mystery woman sooner rather than...never?

Mystery Woman: I suppose I can give it a shot. I should probably sleep first though. Hitting the trail tomorrow morning, and then more family time. Yay.

Luke: Someone kept me up too late, so no pillows on the trail tomorrow either. Sleep tight.

After that message, he set his phone down. He didn't need to wait for a goodnight message from her. He'd heard all he needed to.

She was going to come into his shop for a smoothie.

Now, all he had to do was wait.

And guess.

And wonder who in the world his mystery woman was.

9

*W*ith another successful and beautiful trail hike done, Hannah headed back to the sanctuary. There, she showered in the tiny bathroom, got dressed, and then braced herself. If this day was going to be like the previous ones, Luke would be there shortly.

Somehow, Text Message Guy had convinced her to give Main Squeeze another shot. She hadn't mentioned that she'd had a bad experience there. Brooke had warned her that word got around town quickly, and even though she'd been treated unpleasantly, she didn't want his business to suffer. Not at all. Plus, Brooke kept reassuring her that Luke wasn't the guy he was portraying himself as.

And, honestly, Hannah had to concede that.

Because there he was.

Bright and early that morning.

Ready to volunteer his time so she could get back home.

With his adorable dog in tow.

"Looks like the pigs are happy here," Luke said, approaching her from his car.

She walked over to meet him while Ralph met up with Stella

out in her pasture. It seemed to Hannah like the dog was getting a little attached to the cow, but Stella didn't seem to mind Ralph's attention. Maybe she even liked it.

"Yeah," Hannah replied, slipping her fingers into the back pockets of her jeans. Her thick braid bounced over her shoulder as she glanced at them. "So far so good. They're adorable out there, and I think Stella is happy for the company."

"She's probably just glad it's not Ralph."

As they both watched the dog run up to Stella, back away slowly, and then trot right over to her again, they laughed. When Ralph curled up into a ball at Stella's feet while the cow ate her breakfast, Hannah caught Luke's reaction from the corner of her eye. She couldn't quite read the emotion, but she could tell how much he loved that dog.

Which reminded her about Text Message Guy and how much *he* loved *his* dog.

There was something about a man who could get vulnerable about animals. There really was.

Jack had never been like that. And she hadn't thought Luke would be that way, but there she was, having to swallow that maybe she'd been wrong about the man standing next to her.

Well, did she *really* have to accept that? What difference would it make once she was gone? She shook that thought off just before Luke spoke up.

"So, where's Brooke? She's usually the one pulling out the red carpet for me."

Hannah heard the silent *not you* in there even though he hadn't said it. Part of her felt guilty for making him feel like that, but another part of her thought he could have been nicer in the first place. "She's napping."

Luke's hand flew to his heart as he feigned hurt. "Napping? When you're in such a rush to get back home?"

She gave him a playful shove. "I already told you I was

grumpy that day. Someone was a little rude when I tried to order a salad, so I had to eat fries for dinner, remember?" Laughing lightly, she started heading over to the barn. "But I'm sorry for that."

On her way over, she mentally decided she'd help him paint the barn. It wasn't ideal, but it'd get the job done. Then he wouldn't have to come back. She and Brooke could work together to get the rest of it done before she left on Sunday. It was Wednesday, so four days would be plenty.

Plenty of time to get to know Text Message Guy some more, a small voice in her head said.

Or Luke, it added.

She rolled her eyes at herself. If anything, she should *not* help Luke so that it all took longer and she'd have no choice but to stay. Then it would be out of her control and she'd get to message Text Message Guy as if it meant something.

"All right. I'll take this side, and you—" When she glanced to her side at Luke, her words died off. He wasn't there.

He was where she'd left him, his mouth hanging open in shock. "Did you just apologize?"

A smile she couldn't stop unfurled on her lips. She crossed her arms over her chest, faking annoyance. "If I did, can we call it a truce so we can get this barn painted?"

In surprise, his eyebrows rose. "You're going to help me today?"

She nodded, barely keeping another eye roll to herself. She wasn't bothered though. This was actually kind of fun, bantering with him.

Imagine that, that stupid voice said.

His arms flared out to his sides and then slapped against his legs. "Sure. Let's do this."

She didn't think he seemed annoyed, either, but she didn't want to read into it too much. Instead, she divvied out paintbrushes and cans and they got busy painting the barn in companionable silence.

Comfortable silence.

Enjoyable silence, even.

She kind of liked having company that wasn't just her cousin. Not that she didn't love Brooke. She most certainly did. Otherwise, she wouldn't have agreed to manual labor for a full week. It was a refreshing break to not only have someone else to work beside, but for it to be Luke and they weren't fighting. Just working together to achieve a common task and staying quiet.

Until he spoke up.

"So," he said, "still on track to go home according to plan?"

"Yep." She dipped her paintbrush into the paint and swept the bristles against the wood.

Luke was quiet for a moment, perhaps not expecting a one-word answer. Then he tried again. "Can I ask why you want to leave so badly?"

On a downward stroke, she shrugged. "I just like being at home. Is that a crime?"

"Of course not," he replied quickly. His brush colored the barn as he spoke. "I just don't think it's all that bad here."

"That's because you live here. Of course you like it. You chose to be here."

"You don't think you could like it if you chose to live here?" he asked.

Immediately, she answered with, "No."

"Because you have more family back home than you do here?"

This time, she didn't have an immediate answer. She had to think about that. Did she have more family back in Vermont or there in True Love? Even though the answer was obvious, it shocked her.

"Actually," she said, "no. I don't."

"Boyfriend? Husband?"

She scoffed before she could help it. "No." Then she kept her gaze to herself so she couldn't see his reaction to that.

He stayed quiet for a moment, which made her want to peek, but she didn't. "Friends?" he finally asked.

"A few," she mumbled, stuck in her head.

He also seemed shocked by her words. He peered over at her for a moment before going back to painting. "Okay... Then is it your job?"

These questions made her brain hurt, if she was honest. She squinted as she thought this over. "No, I can do my job anywhere."

Instead of faking like he was more interested in painting, he stopped and faced her. "Then I don't understand. It's not family, and it's not your job. So what's back there that's so important to rush back to?"

She stilled her brush for a moment as that question washed over her. She wasn't sure it had anything to do with Vermont personally. Just that it wasn't...small. Claustrophobic. Cramped. Between staying in Brooke's tiny home and feeling stuck in this small town, she couldn't wait to be back at her own house.

Within minutes of a Target.

Within blocks of a Whole Foods.

Within steps of a blender to make her own smoothies.

But this question... It didn't feel like he was asking about those things. He was asking about something deeper. Something he perhaps had there in True Love that she didn't back east.

Sooner than she could answer, he said, "Sounds to me like you have just as much here as you do there." Then he shrugged as if he hadn't just tilted her world off its axis. "This place is pretty great once you settle in."

Hannah couldn't tell if she believed him for herself, but she knew deep down that he truly believed that for his own life there. This conversation had turned too serious though. This wasn't up for debate. She had her return ticket ready to go, though she'd have to try for standby to leave a week early. She was heading back, no ifs, ands, or buts about it.

She opened her mouth to tell Luke as much, but the sound of a vehicle pulling up at the sanctuary caught her attention first. When she spun her torso around, she found not one but three cars lining up along the edge of the property. And when those three cars resulted in eight people, her brow creased in confusion.

"Who are these people?" she asked.

Luke narrowed his eyes to get a good look. "Mateo?" he called out. Then he strode over to the crowd.

Hannah followed behind, wondering who Mateo was and why he'd shown up with so many guests. The sanctuary wasn't open for visitors yet, and with Brooke sleeping, Hannah didn't know what to do.

Luckily, Luke seemed to have it handled. "What are you all doing here?"

"You said you weren't going to get everything done on time," the man Hannah assumed to be Mateo said. Actually, he looked like a kid, maybe twenty at most. "So I rounded a bunch of people up to come help out." That was followed by a shrug like this was no big deal.

Just a normal day around True Love, Arizona.

Eight people with nothing else going on and plenty of time to donate.

Totally business as usual.

Luke looked over at a confused Hannah, his expression telling her that that was *exactly* what was going on. "I told you this town was pretty great, didn't I?"

Then he winked at her.

Freaking *winked* at her.

Like it wouldn't make her heart flutter in her chest.

Like it wouldn't make her rethink her stance on this town for the second time in as many days.

Like it wouldn't change her hasty decision to leave so fast.

Hannah didn't know what was happening, but experiencing the magic of this town was doing a number on her. One she wasn't sure what to do with just yet.

10

*L*uke had just said goodbye to Mateo when a strange burst of customers came into his shop. On a Thursday afternoon, he didn't usually see this many people. But it wasn't like he was mad about it. Quite the opposite. He was in his element when he had a line nearly out the door.

Usually.

Most days, he didn't have to wonder if one of his customers was Mystery Woman.

Would she have told him she was coming in? Or would she wait until after her visit to tell him? He had no idea. And worrying about if his customers were the person on the other end of his text messages nearly had him messing up orders.

Luckily, he managed to get them right and please his customers.

After the final person in line received their drink, Luke took a deep breath. *This.* This was what it was all about. Giving back to a community with healthy food. Serving the people. Finding his purpose. He thrived off running this business, so he was happy when someone else walked in. The rush wasn't quite over yet, and he had time to pull it together.

When he caught sight of the woman who'd entered his shop though, he had conflicting feelings.

Feelings that said he liked what he was seeing even though he shouldn't.

"What are you doing in here?" he asked, genuinely curious as Hannah reluctantly strode to the counter.

"Well," she started, her palms pressed together in front of her, "I seemed to have some extra time on my hands today because the sanctuary somehow had a whole slew of volunteers who got a lot of things done. The goat pens have been built, the barn has a fresh coat of paint..." She shrugged as the corners of her lips slowly tilted up into a hint of a smile. "There was nothing left for me to do but give this place another shot."

"Ahh," he knowingly replied. "Not many other options out there anyway, huh?" He returned that grin.

She let out a small laugh. "There is that." Then she braced her hands on the edge of the counter while he cupped his around the computer screen of his register. "But someone also convinced me to try again, so I thought I'd stop by."

With one finger, he tapped the screen. "Your cousin is a really good person. She must be very persuasive."

Hannah's mouth opened as she sucked in a breath, but it closed a second later. Whatever she'd been about to say about Brooke was gone. "So, what kind of green juice is best here?" She eyed the menu, drumming her thumbs on the counter.

Luke glanced over his shoulder as if he didn't have the whole thing memorized. But with Hannah's new approach with him, he'd been caught off guard. "Let's see... I mean, *all* of them are good. Otherwise, they wouldn't be on the menu."

When she rolled her eyes, that cute grin returned.

The one he was getting used to.

The one he liked more than he should.

He wanted to close his eyes so he couldn't see it anymore,

but his heart wouldn't let him. Instead, he managed to focus on the screen while his fingers tightened around it.

"Which one do you think I'd like?" she asked.

He had no idea, so he went with his usual questions for regular customers. "Well, are you allergic to anything?"

"Just pineapple."

At that, his head twitched backward. "Really?"

She nodded. "Yep. It's a thing and it's sad because it's really delicious."

"Then I'd suggest one without pineapple..." he said, but his voice trailed off when he recalled another recent conversation about pineapple.

Which make him think about Mystery Woman and who she was again.

Hannah replied, breaking him from those thoughts. "It looks like one of them has pineapple, so I'll take one of the other two. Doesn't matter which."

"Right. Got it." He pushed away from the computer screen and grabbed the ingredients he needed to make her juice. But his mind wouldn't stop whirling.

That mention of pineapple led him to wonder if...

No. It couldn't be.

Mystery Woman had said she didn't put pineapple on pizza —not that she was allergic. And she wanted to come in for a smoothie, not juice. But other things added up. Like the fact that she was here from out of town. Visiting a cousin. Into healthy food. Looked like she'd exercised in the morning just like Mystery Woman did on the trails.

All he could do was blink as he tried to reconcile those text messages with the woman standing in his shop.

No way.

"I have to run to the back," he told her. "We're out of spinach up here."

Hannah nodded. "No problem."

She didn't react to the mention of spinach, so maybe it wasn't her. But there was only one way to check.

Once the door to the back had swung closed, he took his phone out of his pocket. He pulled up his text message thread with Mystery Woman and started typing. If she checked her phone or he heard a beep when he sent this, he'd have his answer.

Luke: So did you end up going to Main Squeeze? Or do you only take my hiking recommendations seriously?

He pressed send, his heart in his throat. Then he grabbed the spinach he hadn't actually needed and returned to the front.

No beep. No buzz. No movement from Hannah.

Nothing happened.

So...it wasn't her.

Or maybe her phone was on silent. He'd watch until she left to see if she'd check her phone. It could still be her.

A moment of panic hit him with that thought. Did he actually *want* it to be her? They hadn't gotten along very well. Maybe they'd simply gotten off on the wrong foot, but still. In the end, she'd go back to wherever her home was and he'd still be there. The same would happen with Mystery Woman anyway, so a part of him hoped she never responded. He should probably stop all of this before it went too far.

"Found the spinach?" she asked in a pleasant tone.

"Yep." He bobbed his head and then got to work on her juice.

As the juicer roared, his mind did the same. Too many questions swirled around in his brain.

What would he do if Mystery Woman turned out to be Hannah? He really liked messaging with her. Chatting with her had become one of the highlights of his stressful week. Even though Ralph was on the mend, knowing that Hannah had seen a bad side of him had been eating at him. He'd tried to apologize and make it up to her by doing what she'd asked, but it was probably too late.

And, he reminded himself, she was leaving. He couldn't get that huge fact through his head.

Before he knew it, her juice was ready. He put the lid on her cup and nabbed a paper straw from the holder on his way back to the counter. He had to let all of these questions and thoughts go. All it was doing was stressing him out more, and he needed to stay focused on his business so he didn't lose this one like he had before.

"Here you go," Luke said as he handed it over. "Hopefully it doesn't suck."

Hannah let that genuine giggle loose, which brought all of those questions and thoughts right back into his head. "I'm sure it doesn't. Can't be worse than anything else I've eaten this week." Then she dug into her purse.

Which made his heart stop.

What if she checked her phone and found his text? Would she reply? Be happy to have heard from him? How would he feel about that?

None of that mattered when all she did was pull her debit card from her wallet.

He pushed it back toward her. "No way. The least I owe you for being rude to you the other day is a free drink."

She cocked her head to the side. "Except then I was rude back and basically demanded free manual labor so I could get home sooner." Shoving her card in his direction, she insisted, "Seriously. It's the least *I* can do."

See? This was exactly why he shouldn't have told Mystery Woman to come to his shop. Now, he had suspicions that it might be the one person in the world it shouldn't, and he couldn't stop himself from wanting it to be her now.

This was not good.

Stepping away, he said, "Nope. It's on the house. I insist." Not because he wanted Mystery Woman to see him on his best behavior. Or Hannah for that matter. He just wanted to get back to being the guy he was deep down.

Not someone who snapped because his dog was sick.

Someone who genuinely cared about others and fit into this town full of helpful, compassionate people.

It was why he'd moved there when things had gone south in Tucson. He needed to be that person again.

A grateful pout graced her face. "Thank you, Luke. That's really kind of you. And, if I'm honest," she said, sliding her debit card back into her wallet, "not unexpected. I guess Brooke was right about you."

His mouth went dry as any response evaporated from his tongue. She'd talked about him with her cousin?

Still facing him, Hannah started her approach toward the door. Lifting her drink in the air, she said, "Thanks for this. And just...thank you in general."

"For what?" he asked.

She shook her head as if she didn't know what to say. But that wasn't the Hannah he knew. That Hannah had a reply for everything, so this new side of her interested him.

Finally, she found the words. "For this morning. Getting those people to the sanctuary to help out."

"Oh," he replied. It was now his turn to shake his head. "I had nothing to do with that. That was all Mateo."

A quiet, calm expression softened her features. "Sure, but you must have said something to him about volunteering there."

"I didn't ask him to bring people there though."

"I know," she said. Her hands gripped her cup as she peered down at it. Then she brought her gaze back to him, warming him as though it were full of sunshine. "But it showed me why you love this town so much. Why Brooke had one of her 'feelings' about this place." After a pregnant pause, she finished with, "I think I get it now."

A tightness he hadn't even noticed in his chest loosened as he watched her make that connection. It was one of the most beautiful things he'd ever seen.

"Anyway, thanks again." She shrugged and held her drink up. "You really didn't put any pineapple in this, right?" A smirk teased her lips.

He lifted his hands in surrender. "Nope. No pineapple. I aim to please my customers—not kill them."

"Oh, it would have only given me hives," she informed him. "My arms would have been itchy for a few days. That's it."

His eyes widened as his eyebrows rose. "Oh, well, in that case, I'll remember that if you demand free manual labor again." Then he winked at her like he had at the sanctuary that morning. He was becoming fond of that move, apparently.

She laughed again, the sound like music to his ears. If he wasn't careful, he'd become addicted to that sound.

"See you tomorrow, then?" she asked, her back right up against the door.

He nodded. "Yep." Then he waved and she pushed her way out onto the sidewalk.

Through the glass, he watched her, hoping she'd reach into her bag again for her phone. Maybe she'd check it, find his text, and smile. But maybe she'd check it, find his text, and ignore him. Honestly, he wasn't sure which option felt worse.

He couldn't fall in love again. Not with someone who wasn't sticking around. Not when his business was finally off the ground again. Not while Ralph was sick.

The timing was terrible.

The questions were unending.

But Luke couldn't deny how he was feeling even if he wanted to.

What he did need to do was take back his affirmative answer. No, he wouldn't be there tomorrow. He'd forgotten about his job —the one thing he could not forget about under any circumstances—when under the spell of the hope in Hannah's voice. She'd sounded like she actually *wanted* to see him tomorrow, which was a total one-eighty compared to day one.

When he finally snapped out of his thoughts, he raced to the door, hoping he'd catch her to explain why he wouldn't be there the next day. She was gone though. Reaching into his pocket for his phone, he figured he'd send her a text. But then he realized he didn't have her number. Not for sure anyway

And even though it was a dangerous idea, he wanted to change that as soon as possible.

$\mathcal{B}$y Friday morning, Hannah hadn't heard back from Lucy. She decided to reach out to her again to make sure she'd received her email. With the time on the East Coast being three hours ahead, she was sure Lucy would see it right away.

Even if Lucy replied quickly, that wouldn't explain why she had no other emails in her inbox.

Had all of her clients abandoned her? One vacation to volunteer for her cousin and they'd all jumped ship? She sincerely doubted that. Logic told her that that was pretty much impossible. She was a great coach; her clients told her that all the time. They wouldn't have up and left her like that.

But her lack of emails worried her anyway.

To combat that, she fired off a message to all of her clients just in case. She wanted them to know she was there for them even if she was out of town.

When nothing showed up within a minute, she trusted that they'd get back to her if they needed her. Then she powered her computer down and snagged her phone off the kitchen sink. She hadn't heard from Text Message Guy since the day before, so perhaps something was wrong with all of her electronics. Surely everyone wasn't ignoring her, right?

Hannah: Didn't get out on the trails this morning. Had to catch up on some work. But I did give Main Squeeze a go. Thanks for that recommendation. You've been so spot on.

After sending that text, she noticed that it was almost six a.m. Luke had been showing up at that time on the dot each morning, and the thought of him arriving soon had her...

What?

Excited? Nervous?

Things had gone well at his shop the day before. Really well. They'd even exchanged a little banter. He had a sense of humor —imagine that. She was starting to see what Brooke had seen in him.

Maybe even a bit more than that.

Oh, who was she kidding? Definitely a bit more, seeing as Brooke only had eyes for Kyle, the ice cream guy.

It was hard to reconcile her first impression of Luke with the man she was getting to know, but it wasn't impossible. She certainly hadn't shown him her best behavior at first. And she'd been trying to be nicer, friendlier, more patient. More like the other people in True Love.

When her phone's clock struck six, she marched out the door of Brooke's tiny home. Much to her dismay, Luke's car wasn't ambling up to his usual parking spot. Ralph wasn't bounding out the driver's-side door and over to Stella. The man himself wasn't winking at her when he arrived.

He wasn't there.

Hannah sat on the steps up to Brooke's house and wondered if Stella would miss Ralph if they didn't show up. She'd thought Ralph was annoying the cow, but even Stella craned her head to check for their car.

Both women were ultimately disappointed.

Brooke noticed when she left the pig pen and took a seat next to her. "What's up? You okay?"

"Do you really have to ask?" Hannah gave Brooke a side-eye glance. "Aren't you having one of your 'feelings'?"

The sly smile on her cousin's face answered that clear as day. "That doesn't mean I don't want to hear you say it."

"Say what?" Hannah chuckled even though she was kind of annoyed with the whole situation. "That you can tell me, 'I told you so'? I don't think so."

"Does that mean someone finally sees the real Luke and not the guy he was for one minute nearly a week ago?"

Hannah started to speak, but she didn't know how to answer that. Yes was the short version. But the longer version was that she'd seen the real Luke the moment she'd stepped into the juice bar.

The backwards cap holding his hair back.

The white T-shirt pulled taut over his muscles.

The three-day-old scruff that perpetually stayed the same length.

She'd liked those things the second she'd seen him. But looks weren't everything. Jack had taught her that well. Handsome though he'd been, he hadn't shown her the support she'd needed. Or the love. Or the kindness. He hadn't opened up at all.

Luke, however.

He'd shown emotion.

Maybe she hadn't liked it at first, but at least he hadn't been the human equivalent of a cardboard cutout.

"Maybe," Hannah answered, staring out into the spot where his car should have been.

Brooke bumped her with her shoulder. "Well, I'm not surprised."

Of course she wasn't, Hannah thought. Other people's lives didn't shock her. Brooke might not have been able to see things coming in her own life, but she was rarely taken by surprise with the events in someone else's. Hannah had no problem believing that Brooke had seen this coming from a mile away.

She only wondered why she hadn't.

She was so good with helping other people in their lives. Why wasn't hers easier to read?

That thought scattered when her phone pinged in her hand. She bolted into action, going straight for the notification and trying hard to ignore the buzzing in her chest.

"Is that Luke?" Brooke asked, peeking a little over at Hannah's phone.

Hannah shook her head. "No, I don't have his number."

"A client, then?"

"No," Hannah answered, a smile curling her mouth.

Text Message Guy: Working on vacation? I don't think you understand what that word means. Maybe you need more of my recommendations to keep you busy.

Hannah: Haha maybe. But I'm here to work anyway, so it is what it is. Getting juice and hiking are my only breaks.

Text Message Guy: And talking to me.

A giggle bubbled up from Hannah's chest before she could hold it back, which caused Brooke to poke her in the arm.

"Who *is* that?" Brooke asked. "I haven't heard you laugh like that in...ever, I think."

But Hannah ignored her and went back to her texts.

Hannah: Well, I was worried that was over when I didn't hear from you yesterday. Everything okay? How's your dog?'

Text Message Guy: He seems a lot better, actually. Thanks for asking about him.

Text Message Guy: As for me, I'm fine. Busy day at work yesterday. That's all. Same today, so I'll catch you later. Don't work too hard on your vacation, you hear me?

Hannah: Yeah, yeah. *wink*

"All right," Brooke said, breaking Hannah's concentration. "Fess up. I wanna know all about this."

"Wanna talk about what happened with you and Kyle the other day?" Hannah asked.

At that, Brooke slammed her mouth shut and stood.

"Thought so," Hannah told her, raising a knowing eyebrow.

She hadn't thought Brooke would want to open up about that. Her cousin was a fairly private person no matter how open she seemed. She wanted to help the world but couldn't talk about her own life. It made sense to Hannah in a way. She'd coached a few people like that.

Facing Hannah, Brooke put her hands on her hips. "Nothing's going on between me and Kyle." She threw a hand into the air to stop Hannah when she started to protest. "My focus is here, on the sanctuary, and that's that. But you." Tilting her head, she put that hand back on her hip. "Your focus is all over the place. On your phone, on Luke... What's up?"

At first, Hannah didn't want to say anything. She wanted to keep all of this to herself. But keeping things to herself meant she never got fresh eyes on the situation. Coaching other people had helped her realize how beneficial that could be, and she didn't have that with anyone else. Maybe Brooke could be her voice of reason.

She sucked in a breath and then let it all out. "Remember how I texted Sylvia for trail recommendations while I'm here?"

Brooke nodded. "Yeah. You've been hiking nearly every morning, so she's been helpful."

"Yeah, well..." Hannah rose from the steps and started walking over to Stella's barn. On the way there, she told Brooke, "It's not actually Sylvia."

Brooke furrowed her brow as she kept pace next to Hannah. "Then who is it?"

The corner of Hannah's bottom lip pulled down and she

splayed her hands in front of her. "Actually, I don't know." Then she lifted her shoulders, and when they fell, she dared to peek over at her cousin.

Her eyes were wide, her forehead crinkled. "You don't know who you've been texting?"

Reluctantly, Hannah shook her head.

Brooke's eyebrows drew down in confusion. "But you're still texting this person? And you seem to look forward to their messages."

"That's the crazy part!" When they reached the barn, Hannah found Stella lying down in the corner. She and Brooke sat next to the cow, and Hannah stroked the animal's massive side. "I have no idea who the person on the other end is except that he's a guy who lives here in town. But he loves dogs and has a funny sense of humor, so we've had fun sending messages back and forth."

"That's not crazy," Brooke told her.

"No? You don't think that's weird?"

After shaking her head, Brooke stayed quiet for too long. Hannah got the impression that her cousin was having one of her feelings, which worried Hannah for herself. Was her cousin rubbing off on her now that they'd spent a lot of time together?

Finally, Brooke spoke. Her words were quiet and contemplative. "Maybe this town's magic is working on you after all."

Hannah let those words wash over her. Could that possibly be? Was she falling in love with a mystery man? With Text Message Guy? Was that even possible?

No, she decided. No, it wasn't. She didn't know him from Adam. And they were friends.

But what about—

"No," she ultimately said. Not because she believed it, but because she *had* to believe it.

Again, Brooke was silent for a while. Several long, drawn-out beats. Hannah focused on petting Stella and soaking up the cow's calm nature. But that calmness broke when Brooke's voice cut through the silence of the barn.

"You're not sure."

Hannah whipped her head in her cousin's direction. "No, I'm totally sure. The town's lore isn't coming true for me."

All Brooke did was make Hannah uncomfortable with how long she was staring at her. Hannah knew what that meant too. One of Brooke's "feelings" had popped into her head. It made Brooke latch onto Hannah's arm and squeal in delight. However, Hannah wasn't going to feed into it.

She didn't know what her cousin was feeling, but this time, she wasn't sure Brooke was wrong. None of this had anything to do with Text Message Guy. They were just friends like she'd said.

But Luke? No, she wasn't sure about Luke.

That's what scared her the most.

12

*A*t the grocery store, Luke reached for the organic pink lady apples. He appreciated the selection there, even if it wasn't a Whole Foods or Natural Grocers like he was used to in Tucson. Especially since he'd somehow let the juice bar run out of apples.

In his hope not to drop the ball on his business, he'd nearly done just that.

Of course, this was just apples. Just one little thing. But one little thing turned into two, which turned into big things, which made businesses fall apart.

He needed to take a step back and breathe.

Remember why he was doing this.

Keep the reasons Hannah / Mystery Woman couldn't get into his head in the forefront of his mind.

That's why he hadn't texted her. He'd been too caught up in thinking they might be the same person that he hadn't wanted to risk it. Knowing Hannah in real life made the whole thing too dangerous.

If he knew how beautiful Mystery Woman really was in addition to all of her other great qualities...

If he knew how it felt for her to be in his arms.

That she had the capacity to apologize for her wrongdoings.

And that she might be interested in him too.

Then he might be in big, big trouble.

And running out of apples was just the beginning of that.

He shook himself out of those thoughts and palmed a second apple. All of them looked ripe and delicious, and he was sure they'd make good juice. But they were more expensive than they would have been if he'd remembered his bulk order from his supplier. Hopefully this was a lesson learned and he'd do better in the fall when he could order direct from the local orchards.

Don't let gorgeous, funny, kind, smart women distract you, Luke. You know what happened before.

He reached for a third apple, but this time, he didn't feel the smooth skin of a pink lady. Instead, he felt the smooth skin of another kind of lady. The kind that came with long hair, a big heart, and an attitude he was starting to find irresistible.

"Hannah?" he asked without taking his hand away.

She left hers under his when she said, "Hey, Luke." But that lasted only a moment before she yanked it away like she'd been burned. "Grocery shopping?"

"Getting supplies for the juice bar," he answered slowly.

"Ahh." She raised her eyebrows, keeping her gaze firmly on the apples as she picked a couple.

They'd been in each other's presences for two point eight seconds. What could he have already done wrong?

Then he remembered.

"Oh, hey," he started, pushing his cart to keep up with her while she walked away from him. "I'm really sorry I wasn't there this morning. I know I told you I would be, but I... I..."

What was he going to say to her? That, in the heat of the moment with her in his shop, he'd gotten so caught up in her

that he'd forgotten about work? That was the truth. He'd wanted
to see her and be there for her. But forgetting about work had
gotten him in a lot of hot water before. If he'd had her number,
he would have at least texted her.

A small voice in the back of his head thought he actually had
it already, but he didn't want to go there without definitive proof.
And the last thing he wanted to do was embarrass her by asking
that question.

If he was honest, he'd admit that he liked chatting with
Mystery Woman too much, just as a friend, to ruin it. Plus, he
didn't want to ruin whatever he was building with Hannah.

Whatever he'd *been* building, that was.

She whipped around to face him in the middle of the
vegetable aisle. "You what, Luke?" she pressed, fixing him with a
hard stare.

The truth balanced on the tip of his tongue. One movement
could have the words tumbling from his mouth. The idea that it
could destroy things made him want to pivot in another direction. He didn't get the chance though.

She deflated from her rigid stance, her head falling forward
as she jostled the basket in her arms to keep a hold on it.
"Look, it's fine. You don't owe us anything at the sanctuary, and
you've been such an amazing help already. I just..." As she
trailed off, she raised her gaze a centimeter at a time until it
met his.

The heat and vulnerability of it nearly took his breath away.
"You what, Hannah?" he asked, mimicking her question from a
moment ago.

This time, the truth appeared to be on the tip of her tongue.
For a moment, he wondered if they were in the same position:
wanting things neither of them had any business wanting.
Yearning for something that might never work. All she wanted
to do was leave town, and all he wanted to do was keep his busi-

ness this time. But when they were together, those two things seemed impossible to him.

He'd want her to stay, and she'd distract him.

It was inevitable. It couldn't work.

That didn't mean she didn't look like she wanted it to.

After a deep exhale that sounded a little defeated, she let her lips gently curve upward. "I just seem to be used to having you around over there. You know," she added quickly, "like a buffer from Brooke so she doesn't talk me into staying longer again."

"Again?" The world flew out of his mouth, hope dripping from the two syllables.

Hannah nodded. "Yep. I'm here getting more groceries because it looks like I need to be here for another few days at the very least. Her new goat arrivals should have been five in total, but it turns out they meant fifteen."

Luke's eyes grew wide as he imagined fifteen goats wandering around the sanctuary with no real place to stay. Maybe in the barn with Stella for a while? They hadn't built enough pens to hold that many goats.

"Which means we need to add more fencing," she continued, "and I need more food for that."

"Good thing this grocery store has that." He smirked at her.

"Imagine that," she joked before ambling over to the bananas. "It's not Whole Foods, but I guess I shouldn't have judged it too harshly. They actually have a decent organic section."

"Wow." Luke whistled as he followed her. "A girl who can admit when she was wrong. I like it."

She laughed as she faced him, wielding a bunch of bananas in her hands like she wasn't scared of using it as a weapon if she needed to. "Yeah, yeah."

Hannah moved from the bananas to the berries section, but Luke's feet were rooted in place. That same phrase—Mystery

Woman had used it in a text that morning. Combined with her mentioned staying with a cousin and making healthy food choices... He couldn't help but wonder.

True Love was a touristy town, no doubt about it. Lots of people came and went on a daily basis, and enough people lived there that family coming in for a visit wasn't unreasonable.

But too many coincidences were piling up. Too many things led back to the same conclusion.

That they were the same person.

He needed to find out.

"Well, hey. How about this," he suggested. "I have to take these apples to the shop, but we can get you a smoothie for strength—no pineapple, I promise—and I'll go back to the sanctuary with you to help with the fencing."

A grateful grin spread over her face. "Really?"

"Yeah," he confirmed. "I'd be happy to."

Not because he wanted her to leave.

Because he wanted to spend more time with her.

To figure out if she was Mystery Woman.

Not to fall for her even more.

Even though that was exactly what would happen.

FIVE HOURS LATER, Luke's shop had apples again and the sanctuary had enough fenced area for the fifteen new goats. He'd managed to wrangle Ryan, the owner of the local hardware shop, to help them, and he in turn had grabbed Devon, the town's handyman who also helped his fiancée, Penelope, run the inn. They'd scrounged up a bunch of other people—their friends and even a tourist or two—to get the job done.

Just like that, Hannah had the opportunity to go back home on time.

All because of him.

And, well, the town of True Love.

Usually, he'd heard about the town *not* giving people the chance to give up on love. Like it colluded with fate to make people find their soul mates and work things out no matter what.

For him, the town seemed to be giving him every occasion to give Hannah an out. He had to wonder when she'd finally take it.

"Thank you so much," she said genuinely as everyone else who'd helped out drove away. "We really couldn't have done any of that without you." She wiped sweat from her brow with the back of her arm.

A piece of hay was stuck to her skin, and when she pulled her arm away from her face, the hay stayed put on her forehead. It made him chuckle, which wasn't the right response to what she'd just said.

She blinked at him. "What? What's so funny?" With a hand on her hip, she tilted her head. "I thought we were getting along now."

"We are," he chuckled as he took a step toward her. He couldn't have wiped the grin off his face if he'd tried. "But you have something right..." With two fingers, he reached forward to pluck it off her skin.

But she ducked away from his touch at the last minute, swatting at his hand. "What's on me?" she asked, swiping at her forehead. "Is it a bug? Arizona bugs are weird. Get it off me." After a few more attempts, the hay hadn't budged.

"It's not a bug. Hold still." He approached her again with his hand. "It's just"—once he had the hay between his fingers, he pulled it away and showed her—"this. All gone. See? No weird Arizona bug on you."

Then, like a total weirdo, he winked at her. Again.

He had to stop doing that.

Except the way she completely froze and stared at him as though she didn't want him to stop doing that made him never want to miss another opportunity to do it again.

It also made a question he never should have asked fly out of his throat.

"Hey, what are you doing tomorrow night?"

Immediately, a stuttered answer spilled from her lips. "N-nothing. Why? What are you doing?"

"Well, now that these adorable goats have proper fencing and space," he said, inching a little closer to her. Inside, he screamed to himself to stop. He shouldn't pursue this. His business would fail. But for some reason, be it the town's doing or his own morbid curiosity, he kept going. "I was thinking maybe we could have dinner."

He thought maybe she'd seem surprised, ask him why they should do that. He prepared to defend that request. But she surprised him instead by readily agreeing.

"Okay," she answered breathily. Then a moment of clarity hit her. "But don't you dare think of taking me to Carrie Ann's."

"I'll make sure you have vegetables on your plate. And no pineapple, I promise."

At that, they both laughed, some of the seriousness of the situation evaporating. That was another thing he liked about being around her. She knew when to joke to lighten the mood. He hadn't thought it possible with how serious she'd been before, but this side of her was refreshing and stunning. She kept him on his toes, and he liked that. A lot.

Probably too much for someone who'd leave.

But he wanted to know more about this woman. He also wanted to prove to himself that he was right about his suspicions. She was Mystery Woman, wasn't she?

That question would be answered. But it would leave him with another one: What would it mean if she was?

He had no idea. All he knew was that Mateo was working the next day at the shop, which meant he had a day off. That was plenty of time to show Hannah his favorite food spot.

Which was plenty of time for him to ruin everything he'd worked so hard for, but he ignored that. Something about this woman soothed him, made him feel like he could make both work. His job, a relationship—balance. Hannah gave him hope. Hope he hadn't had in a long time. And he wanted to keep that.

All he could do was hope that she'd want that too.

Even after the truth came out.

13

"*I*'d say I can't believe this," Brooke said, "but that'd be a lie."

Hannah knew that her cousin was referencing that "feeling" she'd had the morning before, but that was fine with her. All of this was insane, so if Brooke wasn't warning her off, then she'd go with it.

Go wherever it took her.

Until she had to go back home.

While she got ready for her dinner with Luke, she tried to ignore her cousin. Brooke wasn't having that though, and in the tiny home, it wasn't like Hannah could be all that successful. Brooke kept poking her head into the cracker box bathroom and Hannah had nowhere else to go.

Or did she?

"I could go do this at the inn, you know. I bet Penelope wouldn't bother me the way you are." She'd met the lovely woman while she'd been in town, and even though Hannah thought she might have asked the same questions as Brooke, it would have been easier to push them aside with her.

"You sure about that?" Brooke asked, raising a knowing eyebrow.

Hannah sighed as she smoothed her hands over her hair one last time. "Doesn't matter. I'm done now."

"Well, I think you look great for your date."

"It's not a date," Hannah groaned for what felt like the thirtieth time. "He just wants me to get a good meal in while I'm here. Maybe it's so I don't leave this town thinking all it's good for is juice from a rude business owner and French fries for dinner."

"We both know that's not true," Brooke countered, following Hannah to the front door.

Hannah snagged her purse from the counter and put her heels on. "Oh, you're right. I forgot about this beautiful place you've built." Then she eyed her cousin as she palmed the doorknob. "But that's it."

Deep down, she knew she was lying. It was protection so she didn't get hurt. She knew that too. But uprooting her life for this small town sounded...crazy. Cuckoo bananas, really. She'd never recommend such a thing to her clients, so it wasn't advice she'd take for herself.

"Whatever you say," Brooke singsonged while Hannah pushed through the door. "I guess you didn't find all of that organic produce at the grocery store, then."

At the bottom step, Hannah spun around to face Brooke. "Okay, so the grocery store doesn't suck," she said, cracking a grin.

Brooke folded her arms over her chest and propped a shoulder against the doorjamb. "And the people here don't suck, either."

Hannah had to nod, admitting that was true. "Sure. You're here, after all."

When Brooke opened her mouth to reply, Luke's car pulled

up. Hannah half expected Ralph to come bounding out of it, but the dog wasn't in sight. Instead, a familiar voice filled her ears as Luke got out of the car.

"I wasn't talking about me, Han," Brooke said.

Hannah's heart sped up at that thought. Then she peeked over her shoulder at Luke again and her heart raced harder. She knew exactly who Brooke had been talking about the moment she'd said it. She simply hadn't wanted to acknowledge that.

But now that he was there in person, she couldn't deny it.

Luke didn't suck.

Not at all.

Her heart pounded, needing her brain to catch on to that fact. She wasn't sure she could let it though. Not until his slow, awe-filled once-over the moment he'd approached her.

"Wow," he said, appearing genuinely appreciative of her efforts to look nice that evening. "You clean up pretty well."

Her pounding heart slowed to a shocked thud at his sweet words, but it wasn't those that made that same heart melt. It was the way he was looking at her. As if he couldn't see Brooke or the house or the animals running around the sanctuary.

As if all he could see in his whole world was her.

She didn't want to take notice or make the comparison, but Jack had never, not once, looked at her like that. That made all the difference, her heart told her. Things could be so much different, so much better, if that was how Luke felt about her. Maybe she wasn't making the same mistake a second time after all.

That thought propelled her forward, and Luke came closer to her too.

"You do too," she said, admiring how different—how good— he looked without his backwards cap. She liked that style on him, but this... With his hair styled without being overdone...

This was good. *Really* good.

Just before they reached each other, Brooke called out to them. "Have fun, you two. Don't keep her out too late." Then she winked at them and took off for the goat pens. "Or do. Doesn't matter. I'll be out here making sure these goats feel like they're at home." While walking away, she tossed a wave over her shoulder.

That left Hannah alone with Luke.

She'd been in that position before, but the air felt thicker now. Like more was on the line with them going on this not-date. He was simply being a good friend, showing her that there was more to this town than the things she'd held against it originally.

Though that information could make her want to stay.

Was that his actual plan? Did he want her to make True Love her home?

Inwardly, she groaned. She was getting way too far ahead of herself. They'd eat dinner, she'd keep working at the sanctuary until it was time to go home, and then she'd leave. She'd get back to work and pick up her usual schedule.

"Ready to go?" he asked, breaking her out of those thoughts. When she nodded, he extended an arm toward his car. "Your chariot awaits."

Warmth spread through her chest. She enjoyed his banter and the way he spoke to her. It reminded her of Text Message Guy in that regard, how much fun they could have in their back-and-forth conversations. She appreciated that about Luke, that he wasn't the man she'd pegged him for at first, and he kept surprising her.

"You know," she said as he opened the door for her, "I'm a little disappointed that Ralph isn't joining us tonight." Then she folded herself carefully into his vehicle.

"Actually..." He held a finger up before closing her door. Once he was behind the steering wheel, he started the car. "He is."

"Wow. A dog-friendly restaurant here in True Love?" She was stunned.

This town was so small that she hadn't been expecting that. But the more she thought about it, the more that surprise faded away. This place now had a full-blown animal sanctuary. Of course they were a dog-friendly town.

"You'll see when we get there," he said.

"Well, you can add that to the pro column of staying in True Love," she muttered to herself. But when she replayed those words in her head, she realized what she'd said.

What she'd said loudly enough for Luke to hear, in fact.

She tried to correct herself. "I mean—"

Luke spoke over her as he drove. "Staying? You're thinking about staying?"

"I... I..." Hannah stuttered, trying to think of how to fix this. Nothing came to mind though, so she settled on a generic, watered-down response. "I don't know. I don't know why I said that."

He glanced over at her, but she didn't meet his gaze. Before the silence became too thick and awkward in his car, he said, "Then you wanna talk some more about that pro-con list? I can help you out, add more pros to balance things out."

She countered with, "Who said the pros weren't winning?"

At that, he splayed one hand out, palm up. "I mean, you've had nothing but glowing things to say since you stepped foot in town, so I shouldn't have assumed that." His sarcasm didn't disappoint.

"Okay," she said around a light chuckle, "that's fair." Then she quickly added, "But in my defense, the place is called True Love and I've pretty much sworn that off, so of course it was a bit jarring." When Luke didn't respond right away, she went on. "Plus, there's no Whole Foods."

"I've been saying that too!" he exclaimed next to her. "I could totally use one for the juice bar."

"But didn't you find what you were looking for at the grocery store earlier?" she asked.

"Actually, I did." Then he glanced at her again, the ghost of a smile on his lips. That smile felt like it was hiding something yet telegraphing it loud and clear.

Was he talking about *her*? She swallowed thickly at the idea, her mouth going dry.

"Because, you know," he continued as if he hadn't thrown her completely off, "they *do* have a good organic section even if they're not the fanciest grocery store in the country."

She broke into laughter as she gave him a light shove on the shoulder. "You're so mean to me. You know that?"

"Mean?" he asked like he was really contemplating it. "Or am I teasing? I think I'm teasing."

"Like how boys tease when they have a crush on a girl?" She hadn't meant to ask that, but the words had come out unbidden anyway.

And her heart thudded a slow, uneasy rhythm as she waited for his answer.

At a stop sign, Luke slowed the car to a halt and then eyed her full on this time. No quick glance. No ghost of a smile. Just his clear eyes and a serious yet soft expression on his face. One that made butterflies erupt in her belly.

"Just like that," he said.

HANNAH COULDN'T BELIEVE how easy it was to be around Luke—even after he'd basically admitted he had feelings for her. That's what he'd done, right? Told her that he liked her? That's how it'd sounded to her, but she hadn't asked him to clarify. She was going back home, wasn't she? None of this mattered that much if she lived thousands of miles away.

But she kind of wanted it to matter.

She kind of felt the same way about Luke.

Much to her dismay.

But it felt...good to feel that way. Addicting. Scary. Euphoric in a way.

Goodness, she was getting confused.

All she wanted to do was talk this out with someone. Just like how her clients did with her. She needed an unbiased opinion, so talking to her cousin was out. She wasn't sure who else she could speak with.

Until a thought popped into her head. *Text Message Guy.*

That was when Luke stopped the car in front of a...house?

"I thought you were taking me to your favorite restaurant," she said, peering out the window.

The house was cute. Adorable, even. A sloped roof topped a home that resembled a log cabin. The closest neighbor was several hundred feet away, and the front yard had a gate around it that looked like it extended into the back. All in all, it gave Hannah a Vermont vibe. It felt kind of like...

Home.

"I said I'd take you to my favorite food spot," Luke answered. His voice brought her gaze to him, and he pointed out the window. "This is it."

"This?" She glanced out the window again, the truth hitting her hard and fast. "Is this your home?"

"Is that okay? Ralph's eagerly awaiting your company, and since you requested his, I thought it'd be kind of perfect."

Perfect. Home. Those were words Hannah didn't use often. She had a house in Vermont, and things were acceptable. Maybe not perfect or ideal, but they were hers.

This was a whole new level of perfect and home. And if she

hadn't learned so many coaching techniques for her clients, she might not have known how to handle it. Instead of freaking out, she employed her "count to five and make a decision" technique.

That decision was to get out of the car and get on with this date.

Not date.

Whatever.

Maybe it was now, and maybe she was fine with that. More than fine. She shouldn't have been, but resisting her feelings only made things worse. She'd told her clients that many times. That night, she'd go with the flow. That was her decision and she'd stick to it.

When she nodded at him, the best kind of smile pulled at his lips—a genuine one. One that showed him as the kind, caring man Brooke had described him as. The kind of man she was learning he really was. That smile calmed her racing mind as he helped her out of his car and up to his front door.

Then Ralph obliterated all of her chaotic thoughts by nearly jumping into her arms the first moment he saw her. It made her giggle and wrap her arms around the huge dog. Once they'd both calmed down, she crouched in the foyer and scratched Ralph around his ears.

"Ralph! Buddy. You have to let her in or she's never coming back." Luke winked at Hannah.

The whole scene warmed her heart. He wanted her to come back even though they'd gotten off on the wrong foot. She wanted to come back even though she'd started off with the wrong impression of him. First impressions weren't everything, it seemed. Sometimes, things didn't go the way she wanted them to. Lots of lessons learned there, and she'd take them all to heart, just like she instructed her clients to do.

But the moment Luke walked toward the kitchen saying he would start working on a healthy dinner complete with vegetables, she riffled through her bag to find her cell phone. Then she fired off a text to, at the very least, get her excited feelings out for unbiased feedback. Someone with no skin in the game would be able to tell her if she was being crazy. Even though, deep in her gut, she didn't think she was.

Being there with Luke felt good. Right. Easy.

But a second opinion never hurt.

Hannah: Okay, we're friends, right? So I can tell you that I'm on a kind-of date, maybe not a date, but I think I want it to be a date, right? And I'm still in True Love, so this shouldn't be a thing, right?

She took a deep breath after hitting send on that text to Text Message Guy.

Then she put one foot in front of the other toward her kind-of date.

Okay, it was a date.

14

"So, what are we eating here at your favorite food spot?"

Luke scraped cabbage into a big pot. With Ralph sitting patiently near his feet, he sidestepped to put the cutting board in the sink. "Something called boiled dinner, which I hear is a popular New England dish."

Hannah's mouth fell open. "You didn't."

"Oh, I did," he assured her, walking over an unmovable dog to get back to the stove.

"You Googled it, didn't you?"

"Yep."

She was quiet for a moment, but then, in a soft voice, she asked, "For me?"

He stirred the cabbage in, put the lid on the pot, and set the timer. "So you can have a little taste of home right here in Arizona." Then he took a seat near Hannah at the kitchen table to wait for the food to be ready.

The appreciation written all over her face let him know that he'd made a good choice. "Thank you. Really. That means a lot."

"You've had one foot out the door since you got here, so I thought it was the least I could do."

She shrugged. "I don't know about that. You've gone above and beyond to make me realize some things about 'home,'" she told him, using air quotes. "I think I've reevaluated my position on the matter."

He quirked an eyebrow. "Oh? Does that mean you're staying a little while longer?" He'd wanted to ask about longer than that, but he thought he'd start there.

"Maybe," she said, but the tone of her voice betrayed her real answer: yes. "I'm thinking about it, anyway."

"Well," he asked, crossing ankle over ankle and folding his hands in his lap, looking causal, "how many more boiled dinners do I need to make to convince you of that?"

Her lips split into a grin before she aimed her gaze at the pot on the stove. "I'm not sure. It depends on how good that one is."

"I guess we'll see." Luke got up to check on it. Everything seemed like it was turning out fine. "I hope you like seitan though. I remembered your vegan comment at the juice shop, so I thought that would work."

"You remembered?" she asked, awe tingeing her voice. "That's really sweet."

"Of course. Though we don't eat meat here anyway." He amended that when Ralph lifted his head as though he were wondering if he was included in that. "Well, I don't."

She took a deep breath in through her nose. "That smells so good."

After putting the lid back on, he went back to the table. "I hope it tastes as good as it smells. I've clearly never done this before, so we'll see."

"Well, I trust you. Your juice *was* the best I've ever had."

"Really?" he asked as he sat. "I mean, it's just juice."

Lines formed in her brow as she shook her head in tiny movements. "No, no, no. It's *juiced with love*."

That made him chuckle a little. He ran a hand over the

stubble on his chin and tried to tame his grin, but he couldn't. In Hannah's presence, he did nothing but smile, laugh, and feel good. All of that was addicting, and he wanted more of it. He didn't want this night to end.

"Actually," Hannah said, narrowing her eyes and staring off to the side, "it might have been the second-best juice I ever had."

"Oh really," Luke deadpanned. "Please, do tell about the actual best juice you've ever had."

She scooted her chair closer to the table, getting more serious than he'd been expecting. "I can't remember the name of the place, but a client wanted me to travel to her, so I did. Beforehand, I made sure to Google and see if the city had the necessities."

"Like Whole Foods?"

"Yes," she replied around a laugh. "Just like Whole Foods."

"So, where was this place?" he asked as Ralph realized food wouldn't be ready for a while. The dog sidled up next to Hannah, who didn't think twice about scratching the dog's head and stroking his back.

"It was this little shop in Tucson, and your place actually reminded me of it a little. Cute, quaint. Friendly on occasion." She gave him a sly, sarcastic grin at that.

But he couldn't appreciate that as much as he wanted to. Instead, memories filled his head. "The Juicery," he mumbled, more to himself than to her.

She snapped her fingers, seemingly unaware that he'd mentally checked out. "Yes! That's it. Have you been there?"

For several beats, he allowed those memories to run free. That's all the time he gave them though. He didn't want his past there in the present with Hannah. "I used to work there before I moved here."

Surprise took her features over. "Oh wow, really? This was maybe two years ago. Were you there then?"

Nodding, he said, "Yep. That was right before it closed." Right before his entire life blew up before his eyes.

"Huh." The way she said that made him look up, and when he did, she flicked her gaze to him. "Think we met before, then? How crazy would that be?"

It would have been crazy, all right. Maybe his life wouldn't have exploded the way it had if he'd met her before he'd met Loraine. It probably would have anyway because Hannah had a life in Vermont, not Arizona, even back then. And he might have done the same thing, made the exact mistake, whether it was her or Loraine.

But maybe not.

"Maybe you were nice to me back then," she joked, which broke him from his thoughts.

"I was a nicer guy back then," he said. Then he looked to Ralph, who couldn't have been more relaxed with Hannah's attention. "Right, buddy? Much nicer back then."

"Eh." Hannah lifted her shoulders and let them fall. "You seem pretty nice now. Making me a home-cooked meal I might have eaten at home. Some might call that nice."

"Well, thank you, but let's reserve the compliments for after you've tried the food." He grinned at her before getting up.

At the stove, he prepared their dishes, hoping it was *anything* like what she was used to. Then he brought them to the table, where Ralph sat at attention, patiently waiting for dropped food or scraps.

"It looks perfect!" she exclaimed as steam rolled off the vegetables he'd promised to feed her. "I can't wait to dig in."

"Be honest," he told her while he sat. "But not that honest. I usually make smoothies, not four-course meals."

She cut into the slab of seitan, and the moment it touched her tongue, her eyes fluttered shut and she grinned around her fork. "Oh my goodness," she muttered around the food. "Yes,

Luke. This is wonderful. Just like how my mom used to make it."

"Used to?" he asked, hoping that didn't mean what it sounded like.

"Before she and my dad retired to Florida. Not... She's alive. They both are." Using her fork, she speared some of the veggies. "Living it up on the coast, having a good old time."

"Ahh. So that's why you don't have a lot of family back in Vermont."

"Right," she said. "It's also why I work as hard as I do."

He swallowed a bite of food. "Trying to save up money to move down there with them?"

She shook her head, keeping her gaze down. "No. I just don't have much else to do."

"All the more reason to move here," he hedged, gazing up at her through hooded eyes.

The corners of her lips fought not to tilt up. "It's certainly in the pro column."

Cutting into his seitan, he asked, "What else is in the pro column?"

"Well," she sighed, using her napkin to wipe her mouth. "There's Brooke. The sanctuary. All of those pigs and goats. And Stella, of course."

Ralph nudged Hannah's leg, and if Luke hadn't known better, he would have thought he was getting impatient for food. That wasn't it though, and Hannah seemed to know.

"You too, Ralph. You're most definitely in the pro column," she told his dog, which made his heart skip a beat.

Sure, he wanted to be on that list too, but the woman he was interested in loved his dog. That was...*huge*.

"I guess there's also the not-Whole-Foods-but-close-enough grocery store," she continued, using her fork to gather up another bite. "Oh, and Brooke told me about the coffee shop I need to check out before I leave..." Her teasing glance flicked to him before she ate some more.

He pointed his fork at her. "Don't forget the second-best juice you've ever had."

"Oh yeah," she said, feigning ignorance. "I must have forgotten about that."

Their lighthearted conversation felt comfortable. Companionable. Delightful. He liked seeing her in his kitchen, petting his dog, eating his food, and having a good time. He appreciated her sense of humor and the way they could volley back and forth with sarcasm and teasing. It was exactly his speed, which made him wonder if Hannah and Loraine had nothing in common.

Maybe Hannah wouldn't be so extreme.

Maybe she wouldn't hand him an ultimatum.

Maybe she wouldn't destroy all of his life choices.

She might even complement them.

"You know," he said, pushing some of his food around, "you made a remark about swearing off love."

She sat straighter in her chair. "I did, didn't I?"

"You did, and I did the same right before I left Tucson."

Concern pinched her forehead. "What happened?"

"My...girlfriend," he answered, not wanting to look Hannah in the eye. "She was...intense. Wanted all the normal things, like kids and a dog and a white picket fence. I was working hard to be the man who'd be able to give her those things, even going so far as getting a friend for Ralph."

The dog, so soothed by being curled up next to Hannah, didn't even move an inch.

"But in the end, she wanted more than that. *All* of my time, which didn't allow me to keep my mind on my business. One mistake led to another, which ended up collapsing the store, and she left me. Took the dog. Almost took Ralph."

This time, the chocolate Lab released a deep sigh as though he were glad Loraine hadn't gotten that far.

"Oh, Luke. I'm so sorry." Hannah dabbed her mouth with her napkin. "That's why The Juicery closed?"

He nodded, setting his fork down. "Yeah. So I packed up and moved here. I couldn't handle the failure of it all."

Silence grew between them as he felt the pain of those memories squeeze his heart. Like a vise, it cranked until the soft touch of Hannah's hand landed on his. She'd reached across the table to cover his, and the gentleness caused the vise to loosen.

"You made a good choice. Fighting for Ralph, coming here, opening a new juice bar." She gave him a kind nod. "And that's coming from a life coach."

At that, his eyes widened. "That's what you do?"

In big, slow movements, she nodded. Then she slipped her hand away and lifted her plate. "Yep," she said as she rose from the table. "Except it seems like all of my clients have ghosted me this week."

He stood too, taking her plate. "Did you tell them you're on vacation?"

"I did." She made a gimme motion for his plate before reaching for it. "I can wash these."

"Absolutely not." He gathered the dishes and the silverware and took them to the sink. "Sit back down and relax. I'll say it again: You're on vacation. You're not supposed to worry about dishes or your clients, and you shouldn't work too hard."

She furrowed her brow. "Someone else just told me that."

Luckily, at the sink, he had his back to her, so she couldn't see his Adam's apple bob as he swallowed hard. That someone had likely been *him*. "Well, we both can't be wrong."

"No, probably not."

He worked on filling the sink and scrubbing off the leftovers into the garbage disposal. She went quiet, but he needed that silence to think. That had reminded him of his text thread with Mystery Woman and his earlier suspicions that she and Hannah were the same person. He didn't want to think about that with Hannah at his place, so he turned the sink off. But when he spun toward her, she was right there in front of him.

He froze before he ran into her. "Oh, gosh, I'm so—" he started to say. His apology died off when he realized how close he was to her.

Close enough to...

Kiss her.

That near to her, his breath fled from his lungs. Her citrus-and-hay scent flooded his senses, and her wide eyes locked onto his, holding him captive. Just a breath away from her mouth, he only had to lean a little closer to touch his lips to hers. If he dared.

He wanted to.

His heart wanted to.

But his brain, the rational part of him? His brain wanted him to shut it down.

So he told his brain to shut up.

When Hannah closed her eyes, he pressed forward, eagerly awaiting their lip touch. Would fireworks go off? Would sparks fly? Would his heart want to slam out of his chest?

Would he want to give up his business for her?

That question gave him pause. Even though he'd instructed his brain to be quiet, it clearly hadn't. He tried one more time to let the logical part go and lean toward her. This time though, it wasn't him who ruined the moment.

It was Ralph.

He squeezed his big dog body between the two of them and headed straight for the stove. Hopping up, he almost got his nose close to the top of their leftovers. But before he could, Luke realized what he was doing and dashed in that direction.

"Ralph, no. Down!" Luke told the dog, adrenaline whipping through him.

Ralph pushed off the stove and his paws hit the floor, and not a moment sooner did Luke take a breath.

He'd almost kissed Hannah.

Hannah had almost let him.

Not sure what to expect, he peeked over at her and found her smiling at his dog. Relief settled in his veins. She wasn't upset, freaked out, or running away. Even though they'd been interrupted, she didn't seem worried about what they'd been about to do.

He should have been worried, yet he wasn't.

"Mind if I use the bathroom?" she asked.

"Of course not." He pointed her in the right direction, and once she had ambled down the hall, he managed to exhale. "Buddy," he lamented at the dog, his voice hushed. "I can't believe you did that."

Ralph didn't even fake an apology. Instead, he trotted over to his food bowl, picked it up with his mouth, and brought it over to Luke.

"You're kidding," Luke said.

But he knew the dog wasn't kidding, so he got him dinner of his own. As he scooped the food, he laughed quietly.

As he bent to put the food bowl back on the mat, his phone vibrated on the counter. He hoped it wasn't Mateo telling him there'd been a fire or some other kind of disaster at the shop. It'd be just Luke's luck that everything had gone to crap while he'd been trying to date again. He couldn't put love off forever, but if he had to choose...

He didn't get to finish that thought. The text on his phone wasn't from Luke.

It was from the last person he'd expected a text from in that moment.

He read an older one first before moving on to the new one.

Mystery Woman: Okay, we're friends, right? So I can tell you that I'm on a kind-of date, maybe not a date, but I think I want it to be a date, right? And I'm still in True Love, so this shouldn't be a thing, right?

Mystery Woman: Where are you? Big news!

His stomach dropped to the floor. Was this confirmation? If that big news was that they'd almost kissed, then he'd know for sure.

Mystery Woman would in fact be Hannah, and he'd need to tell her.

Luke: Hey. Here. What's the big news?

His heart pounded out a marathon pace as he waited for her answer.

Mystery Woman: We just had a...moment in his kitchen. I think he almost kissed me!

Luke's entire body froze.

There it was. It had to be her, right?

It would have been too big of a coincidence for it not to be. In a small town, how many people would have been on a date and almost had a "moment" in the guy's kitchen like they had?

Even though it was True Love, where everyone found their soul mates, the chances had to be slim.

His fingers shook as he tried to decide what to say back. He couldn't ignore it—he didn't want to. Yet he had to say something.

Before he could though, another message came through:

Mystery Woman: And oh my goodness, his dog broke it up, but you know what? I almost wish he hadn't.

Luke read that message too many times to count. With each pass over it, his heart sank further and further. Had he misread everything that had happened? She'd wanted it to be a date, yet she almost wished he hadn't kissed her? Did he have bad breath? Had dinner been awful? Was there something in his teeth?

No matter what he did, he couldn't come up with an explanation that reconciled her words with what he'd witnessed. What he'd felt.

Still, he wanted to show up as Text Message Guy for her. She deserved a friend, even if he felt like a liar and a fake.

Luke: Just tell him about your weird spinach art. Then *poof* - no more moments.

He thought he heard a giggle come from down the hall, but he wasn't sure. That's the reaction he'd hoped to get as the mystery texter, but now, as Luke, it felt hollow in his chest.

However, he *was* sure he heard her cell ring after that. Then she answered the phone, asking Brooke if everything was okay.

Clearly, it wasn't.

In a panic, she rushed down the hall. "Luke? Luke! I have to go back home."

"Whoa. What's going on?"

"Something with the goats. We have to hurry!" She bolted toward the front door.

With his heart in his throat, he put the lid on the pot and told Ralph to be good while he was gone. Then he snagged his keys from his pocket and dashed outside, leaving any other feelings inside his house.

Except the one that recognized that she'd finally called this place *home*.

Though, for him, it was probably too late.

15

"Brooke?" Hannah shouted the moment she flung her car door open. She'd never been more thankful that this town was so small than she was right then. It'd only taken six minutes to get from Luke's house back to the sanctuary. "Brooke, where are you?"

Her cousin waved from the farthest goat pen. "Over here!"

The panic in her voice shot ice through Hannah's veins. Something was *really* wrong.

"What's going on?" Hannah asked Brooke. "You didn't say much over the phone."

"One of the goats," she answered, tears clogging her voice. "I think she's..."

Hannah heard the word Brooke didn't want to say. She didn't want to think it, either. Even though it was a part of life, a sad part of animal rescue, it would crush Brooke to have it happen so soon into her new venture. And although Brooke was usually the calm, level-headed one, Hannah knew she needed to be that for her cousin now.

She took a deep breath. "Okay, hold on. One step at a time," she said over the goat's bleating. "What are the symptoms?"

Brooke sniffled as she sat up. "She's breathing heavily, moaning like that"—she pointed to the goat in question, whose loud bleats sounded like she was hurting—"and she keeps getting up and lying down, getting up and lying down. I think she's really uncomfortable or in a lot of pain."

"Okay, good. That's good information." Now, Hannah needed to figure out what to do with it. "Oh!" She snapped her fingers. "We could call Kyle! Remember what happened when he was here delivering ice cream?"

Brooke rose to her feet, looking slightly hopeful. She wiped tears from her cheeks and said, "Oh yeah. He did seem to know something about the animals, didn't he?" When she pulled her phone from her pocket, she stared at it for a moment and then let her arm fall. "Ugh, I don't have his phone number. I could Google the shop number, but I don't know if he's there right now."

Hannah kept her thoughts to herself on that matter. She wished Brooke were better at having those "feelings" about her own life; then, she would have gotten Kyle's number when he'd been there on Wednesday.

But a voice she hadn't been sure she'd hear again that night sounded behind her.

"Actually, I do."

Hannah whipped her head around and found Luke standing ten feet away, looking over the goats as he scrolled on his cell phone. "Can you call him?"

"Already on it," he said before bringing his phone to his ear. "Good thing this is a small town, right?"

Before she could answer, Kyle must have picked up. Luke asked him to meet them there, and then he hung up.

"He'll be here soon."

Another six minutes of fretting and worrying later, Kyle pulled his car up to the sanctuary and rushed over. They'd all been silent, watching over the poor goat. She did look like she was suffering from...something. But Hannah wasn't the animal expert. Brooke was, and she didn't know what was happening.

Hannah didn't really, either, but that applied more to her personal life. Now wasn't the time to clarify things with Luke, to let him know that he could try to kiss her again. It wasn't the time at all.

"Luke? What's going on?" Kyle asked the moment he reached them.

Brooke pointed to the goat, who let out a loud bleat.

"Ahh." He rushed over to the goat. "How long has she been like this?"

After checking her phone for the time, Brooke said, "About a half hour, maybe forty-five minutes." Then she paused, biting her lip. "Is she...dying?"

Kyle did a double take at Brooke and put his hands on his hips. "They didn't tell you how far along she was?"

Brooke's face pinched as she tilted her head. "How far along?"

"Yeah," he answered slowly, nodding in the same speed. Then he went over to her and put his hands on her arms. He dipped his head to get her attention. "She's not dying. She's going to be okay. She's just having a baby."

Brooke's eyes flew wide open as shock spread over her face. "She's pregnant?"

"In labor, actually," he answered, the slight hint of a smile on his lips. "She's going to be fine, but we have to help her, okay?" Then he looked at Hannah and Luke. "Can you guys get some towels, floss, and latex gloves?" Rolling his sleeves up, he looked ready to help a goat give birth.

Just like that.

Hannah barely had time for the relief to settle in before she took off toward the tiny home. The only clue she had that Luke was following her was the crunch of his footsteps over the grass. When she reached the door, he grabbed for it first to let her in, and inside, she paused in the little main hallway, needing to catch her breath.

"You okay?" he asked, his voice low and quiet.

She shuddered as her hand flew to her heart. Then she released a deep exhale to move that energy out of her system. "I'm sure I will be, but that was scary. I've never seen Brooke so... unsure before."

"No?"

Twisting around to face him, she said, "No. She's always so confident. She gets these feelings about things and just knows what to do. I've always been a little envious of that, if I'm honest. I've had to work much harder than she has to figure things out. But that?" She extended an arm to point toward her cousin. "I just hope Kyle can always be here for her."

She also hoped Luke could always be there for her. In that moment, she didn't want to leave her cousin alone out here, but she also didn't want to leave Luke. She knew that the best idea was to stay in True Love, at least for a little while longer, until Brooke got settled. Or maybe until Hannah herself got settled.

Suddenly, she could see a life there. With or without a Target within twenty miles, she could build her career and spend time with the animals. She could help Brooke at the sanctuary when she wasn't seeing clients, and best of all, she could explore this new thing with Luke.

That almost-kiss? She'd wanted it more than anything. She wasn't mad that Ralph had split it up before it'd started. The way he'd been so focused on food was relatable, honestly. Hannah couldn't blame him for that. And she couldn't blame a goat in labor for not being able to finish what they'd started now. It just wasn't the time.

She wondered what Text Message Guy would think when she finally got to tell him about all of this.

"Maybe he will be," Luke answered quietly.

The way he'd said it made hope bloom in Hannah's chest. For her cousin, for the sanctuary, and for her own life.

"Where can we find the towels?" he asked, snapping her back to reality.

Right. A goat was giving birth. Kyle had asked for a MacGyver-like list of necessities, and she was going to find them.

A minute later, they had everything they needed: gloves, towels, and floss. She could easily identify why they needed two of those things, but the third... She wasn't sure she wanted to know.

She found out nearly an hour and a half later, when Kyle used the floss to help tie off the umbilical cord. That wasn't nearly as odd as she'd thought its use would be, so that was good. And the goat and the baby were healthy and doing just fine.

Wobbly legs, knobby knees, and all.

So freaking cute.

Momma took to her baby like it was the most natural thing on Earth, and really, it was. Kyle asked if Brooke had any molasses, but she didn't. However, they knew who wouldn't mind them asking about that so late at night.

Allison, the owner of the coffee shop and bakery called Brewing Affection, was the most likely to have that on hand. Luckily, she obliged the request, rushing over with her own personal stash of molasses for the new momma goat. Kyle got busy mixing it with water to offer to the goat to help her replenish nutrients. For a few minutes, she stayed to admire the brand-new life in True Love, but to give the animals their space, she went back home soon after.

All Hannah could do was admire how much this town came together. No one minded running an errand when it was already dark out. No one cared about having the favor returned or what they'd get out of it. They were selfless, helpful people in that town, and it awed Hannah to her core.

She knew without a doubt that her cousin would fit right in.

But would Hannah?

Could she?

She'd gone there needing the regular trappings of her normal life. But she was on the brink of heading back to Vermont thinking she'd miss the regular trappings of the small-town life.

She couldn't believe it'd happened, but it had. To her, no less.

"Well, mom and baby should be fine," Kyle told them when everything had settled down. "You'll want to get some electrolytes for her, and if they can have their own space for a while to keep everyone else away, that'd be good for them." He rose, brushing hay off his pants. "Plus, you'll want some iodine for the umbilical cord."

Brooke got up too and pointed to the stains on Kyle's polo. "I should probably get you a new shirt while I'm at it," she said. "I'm sure you had no idea what you were getting into when Luke called."

He chuckled softly. "No, I guess not, but it's fine. I'm used to it." As if shocked he'd just said that, he furrowed his brow and backtracked. "Was used to it. It's no big deal." Then he started forward, leaving the goats' pen to go back to his car.

Brooke followed after him, and soon, they were out of earshot of Hannah and Luke.

Luke had stayed throughout the whole ordeal, passing over towels and grabbing new ones when all the clean ones had been used up. He'd been such a huge help when he hadn't been required to be, which was yet another check in the pro column. Even though he hadn't been there as long as people like Allison and Kyle, he had small-town living written all over him. He thrived there, and it hurt her to think about what he'd been through in Tucson.

She'd never do that to him, and she wondered if he feared that happening.

With adrenaline wearing off and the late hour to consider, she figured they could talk about it another time. All she wanted was a good night's sleep now that she knew that everything would be fine around the sanctuary. Brooke would want to spend the night out in the pens with the new family, so she'd have the tiny loft all to herself. She wanted to take advantage of that.

"Well, I should get to bed. Thank you for staying here though," Hannah told him, twisting her hands in front of her. "We really appreciate your help. We definitely needed it."

"Yeah, sure," he replied. "No problem."

"And thanks for dinner." She peered up at him through her lashes. "It was amazing. Maybe you should think about opening up a restaurant that serves four-course meals after all."

He popped an eyebrow, looking amused. "As long as the only main course is boiled dinner and all of my customers are New England transplants, I can't see how that could go wrong."

Light laughter flowed from her throat. Things were so easy with Luke. He had a way about him that diffused any situation —except when he was the cause of it, of course. That thought made her laugh more.

"I should probably go, then," Luke said, jutting his thumb toward his car.

"Yeah, absolutely." Hannah waved him off. "Head back home to Ralph."

He nodded once before turning around.

Before he got too far away, Hannah called out, "Hey, Luke?"

"Yeah?" He spun back around to face her, fisting his keys.

"I'm really glad you were here tonight."

He smiled, but it was muted. "You already said that."

"I know." She stepped forward. "But this made me another thing to add to my pro-con list."

"What's that?" he asked.

She took another step closer, fidgeting with her hands. Nerves flew through her, but she was standing in front of Luke. She could tell him how she felt, right? All she had to do was pretend he was Text Message Guy or her cousin and just say the words.

In the end, her feelings didn't come out. Instead, she said, "This town, how it comes together for its people." Her throat worked as she swallowed over the lump in the back of it. "That's pretty special."

Maybe it was her imagination, but she thought he appeared a little let down. Perhaps he'd wanted her to say what she'd been feeling too. He might have even wanted to finish what they'd started in his kitchen. She knew she did.

Now that she was seriously considering staying in True Love, she wanted to see where this would go with him. They'd both sworn love off before, yet there they were, going on dates and nearly kissing to test the waters.

None of that happened though. He only nodded again and said, "Yeah, it really is." Facing her, he started backing away. "See you tomorrow?"

That idea made her heart flutter. "You're not just saying it this time?"

He chuckled before saying, "No, I'll really be here. How's seven?"

She pinched her lips together. "Maybe you should give me

your number just in case. I don't want a repeat of what happened last time."

All humor fell from his face for a split second. Then he ducked his head, staying silent and stock-still for several seconds. Hannah wondered if that had been too forward of a thing to ask, but that made no sense. He'd asked her out to dinner, cooked for her, and almost kissed her for crying out loud.

His phone number was peanuts compared to that stuff.

"Sure," he finally said, sounding like it'd pained him to do so. Then he rubbed a hand over the scruff on his face, some of his hair falling into his eyes. "Want me to write it down?"

Hannah pulled up the new contact screen on her phone and typed Luke's name in. Then she handed her cell to him and let him punch the digits in. Once that was done, he gave it back to her and raked his hand through his hair.

"Goodnight, Hannah," he said before heading to his car.

For some reason, that felt final. But she had his number now, so she didn't think that'd happen.

"Goodnight," she told his retreating back.

Then she checked on her cousin, who seemed content with the new mom and her baby, so she went into the tiny house and up to the loft. There, she plugged her phone in to charge and let exhaustion from the day's events take her under. She'd explain what happened to Text Message Guy some other time, when she wasn't so tired. And wasn't so confused.

For now, she'd see Luke the next day, and they'd get another clean slate.

16

"Anything else?" Allison asked Luke. "We just took some everything bagels out of the oven. I can throw some of those in for you if you'd like."

Luke only needed half a second to think that over. "They're vegan too?"

She nodded.

"Then sure. Why not?" He handed his credit card over and waited for the rest of his food.

As she handed it over, she said, "Say hello to everyone for me over there. Especially that precious new baby." The love in her expression was clearly evident.

He agreed to do so and said goodbye. Then he walked out of Brewing Affection, hoping breakfast would help smooth things over with Hannah. He was sure she'd soon figure out he was the guy she'd been texting all week—if she hadn't already.

In the car, he nearly chugged his coffee, not caring how hot it was. He required all the caffeine after tossing and turning all night, waiting for the other shoe to drop. How she hadn't already put two and two together boggled him, but she'd probably been busy.

A new arrival at the sanctuary would do that.

He still couldn't believe he'd been there for that, and a part of him was pretty excited to see that baby goat again.

And to see Hannah.

Although he couldn't get a read on her—did she know or didn't she? He wanted to figure it out. Maybe it wasn't too late to come clean first and tell her he was the one on the other end of the text messages. If he could tell her before she realized it herself, he might have a shot. Though, after that text she'd sent him the night before, he wasn't so sure he really did. Unless she simply wasn't ready to kiss him yet, and he couldn't blame her for that.

But he'd been there. He'd felt their connection, how drawn in she'd been. He didn't think he'd misread that, but he'd been wrong about women in the past. He was certainly rusty and wouldn't make that mistake again.

He pulled up at the sanctuary right at seven. Ralph wasn't with him this time, but he'd promised his buddy that he'd bring him to visit Stella some other time. For now, the goats needed some peace, and the last thing Luke wanted was to disrupt anything any more than he already had.

With the bomb he had to drop, he thought it best to leave Ralph at home.

After gathering up the coffee and food, he headed toward the goat pens. There, he found Hannah watching over her sleeping cousin. Brooke's sleep-mussed pixie cut stuck out in every direction, and her limbs were covered in hay. But the animals seemed at peace too, so it was all for the best.

Quietly, he approached the women until he was standing beside Hannah. "Good morning," he told her, holding the coffee out to her. "I thought you all could use sustenance. I don't know if you drink coffee, but if there was ever a time to start..." His words trailed off as he eyed the place where the goat had given birth.

"With a long day of animal sitting ahead of me, this is much needed." She raised the cup in his direction. "Thank you."

"And these," he said as he opened the bag of pastries and bagels. "Food would be good. I know it's not the usual healthy food you eat, but they're vegan, so—"

Hannah cut him off by reaching into the bag and eating the first thing that came out—a bear claw. "As long as it's edible, it's fine by me right now. I'm starving."

His stomach swirled as he watched her take a bite. He should have been hungry too. It was breakfast time, and he was never one to skip a meal. Not when his work included making smoothies all the time. His usual breakfast came through a straw, but he'd never turn down a good pastry, especially the ones Allison made.

That day, however... He had absolutely no appetite.

Especially with caffeine churning through his system now.

"Glad I could help," he said, knowing how much he might upset her with the news he had to deliver. He sucked a breath in to prepare to do just that. "Hey, think we can t—"

"Hannah?" Brooke mumbled. "Is everything okay?" Her sleep-filled voice came out a little slurred.

"Hey, good morning." Hannah crouched as she bit into her donut. Then she patted Brooke's leg. "How long were you awake?"

"Oh gosh, I don't know. I think the sun was starting to come up though." Brooke pushed up into a sitting position and dusted the hay off her hands. With her head, she gestured to Hannah's pastry. "What's that and how do I get one?"

Luke took that as his cue to swoop in. "Here you go. Fresh from Brewing Affection just ten minutes ago."

Hannah turned clear, open, expressive eyes in his direction. "Another thing to add to the pro column."

Even though that was fantastic to hear, his stomach sank.

She didn't know. There was no way she'd figured it out yet, so he'd need to tell her. That was actually a good thing, because if she found out on her own, it'd be so much worse.

He didn't need Brooke's "feelings" to know that for sure.

Brooke removed a bagel from the bag and bit right into it. With her breakfast between her thumb and her forefinger, she used the other fingers on her hand to cover her mouth. Then she muttered through bits of dough, "Oh wow, that's so good," and settled back onto the hay behind her. She happily chewed while the rest of them stayed quiet.

"How's the baby doing?" he asked.

That perked Brooke up. "He's great. I think. I may need to ask Kyle to stop by again, though I'm not sure he'll want to."

"One of your feelings?" Hannah asked before polishing her bear claw off.

Brooke squinted and then shrugged a single shoulder. "Maybe." She left it at that and then took on a lighter tone. "But his mom is good too. She's doing better than I'd be doing hours after giving birth—that's for sure."

"Same," Hannah agreed.

That made them all laugh softly. When a quiet lull settled over them, Brooke finished her bagel and then stood. Some of the hay fell off her skin, but a lot stayed stuck to her clothes. She didn't seem to mind, which was good because her life would be filled with a lot more hay, he thought.

"Did you get Kyle's number?" he asked her. "Gimme The Scoop isn't open yet, so he's probably not there, but I can call if you want."

"Would you?" she asked, exhaustion weighing her eyelids

down. "That'd be amazing. And you know what else would be amazing?"

Hannah put a hand on her cousin's shoulder. "Sleep?" she suggested, a hint of humor lacing the word.

Brooke pointed finger guns at Hannah. Then she answered with, "Exactly," in a drawn-out manner. "Mind keeping an eye on the goats for a while for me, Han?"

"Not at all." Hannah give Brooke a gentle push toward the tiny house. "Get some sleep. I'll be out here."

Brooke's hay-covered skirt swished around her legs as she strode to the front door. Once she'd disappeared behind it, Luke knew he had to act. Drawing this out any longer would only make things worse.

"Mind sitting with me for a while?" Hannah asked. "Eventually, I'll have to get to work on fencing for the separate pen. A motherhood suite, if you will." A soft, playful smile curled her mouth up.

He'd never get sick of that smile.

He hated that he'd be the one to make it fall soon.

He hoped against hope that she'd see the situation for what it was though—a happy coincidence.

"For now though," she continued, "we can call Kyle and see if he thinks we should do anything else for these two. That okay?"

"Yeah, sure," Luke said. "I'll do that and then we can get started on the fencing."

"Thank you." She took Brooke's place on the hay, watching over the resting mom as the hours-old baby goat fed. With a gentle hand, she brushed the soft hair of his side and her face melted into an expression of pure happiness.

She'd fit right in at the sanctuary, he thought. No matter what, he hoped he didn't ruin that.

He put the pastry bag outside the animal pen so goats didn't get to it. Once he'd gotten Kyle on the phone, Luke explained the situation. Kyle stated that he was just about to head that way anyway, so he'd be there in less than ten minutes. After Luke told Hannah that, she craned her neck to peer into the other pen.

"I think Brooke wants that one sectioned off a little under the shade for these two. Any chance you want to get started on that? I can come help in a little bit, once Kyle gets here."

That sounded tempting. It'd give him more time to pretend he didn't have something huge to tell her. But if it helped her and Brooke out, then he should probably do it. They could talk privately while working on it. Or maybe once it was done so it was out of the way before everything blew up.

He wanted to do at least that much for them.

"Sure," he said, and then he entered the other pen to check the space out.

Once he'd gotten a good look, he went into the barn to grab the fencing he'd need. In there, Stella munched on her breakfast. He approached her slowly, wanting to say hi and apologize to her.

"Sorry I didn't bring Ralph today. He wasn't too happy about staying home, but with the new baby..." He shrugged like the cow knew what he was talking about. "I'm sure you understand."

Stella swished her tail in his direction.

He didn't know what to make of that, but he patted her side anyway. When she didn't seem to mind, he did it some more. "Got any advice for me?" he asked. "Any sage cow wisdom on how to handle a delicate situation?"

Stoic as ever, she stayed silent. Her head grazed his shoulder though as though she were pushing him to go back out there and just tell Hannah the truth.

"I know, I know," he said, stumbling backward. He got closer to her and gave her side one last stroke. "Today. I swear. I'll help around here first and then get to it." Then he gathered what he needed to build the pen for the new mom and her baby.

On his way to the pen, he noticed Kyle's car pulling up into the lot. Luke's stomach twisted into a knot as he realized what that meant. It was nearly time to fess up and explain as best he could.

Once in the pen, he put the materials down. Before he got started, he wanted to get his work gloves. He'd kept those in his car, so he strode that way, waving to Kyle as he passed the man. When he had his gloves in hand, his phone rang. He slipped his hand into his pocket to retrieve it and then answered it.

"Hey, boss," Mateo said. "How come the shop isn't open?"

Luke tilted his head. "What do you mean? You have the keys, don't you?"

"Yeah, I do," his employee said, "but I'm not at the shop to open it. It's your day, but someone called to ask why no one was there."

Luke's eyes crinkled at the corners as he thought that over. "No, it's Saturday. That's your day."

"No, it's Sunday."

Crinkles no longer graced his eyes now. They flew open, wide with shock, when he realized they were right. He'd had dinner with Hannah the night before, which had been Saturday. It was now Sunday morning.

And he'd forgotten all about his shop.

All because of the woman currently talking with Kyle in the goat pen.

His chest flared with heat—and not the good kind. "I'll be right there."

Talking with Hannah would have to wait. He had business to attend to. Literally.

The one thing he'd been worried about was back on his radar. He would *not* lose another business because of a relationship. One day, he'd figure out how to do both, but it wasn't that day. He'd dropped the ball and he needed to get to the shop as soon as possible.

Without saying goodbye, he booked it back to his car and drove the few minutes to the shop, thankful he'd moved to a town where that was possible.

Inside Main Squeeze, he flipped the lights on, turned the *open* sign over, and went into the back to get salad dressings ready. Everything else was made to order, and when he checked out the refrigerator to see which dressings he needed to prepare, he found that the answer was...zero.

Everything was ready for the day.

Mateo had made sure of that, it seemed.

After closing the refrigerator door, he put his back to it and let his head fall against the cool steel. A long, deep exhale left him feeling ragged and empty.

He'd made it to work.

His business was fine.

But things with Hannah weren't.

And as much as he wanted to ignore that, a voice inside his head told him that he couldn't.

17

*H*annah opened her arms to give Kyle a hug. "Thank you so much for doing all of that. I know how much Brooke appreciates all of your help."

Kyle hesitated leaving the embrace, and when he finally did, his gaze was aimed at the ground. "I'm not sure I'm ready to make a habit of it, but I'll try."

"Well, thank you again," she said, laying a gentle hand on his shoulder. "When Brooke gets up, I'll have her call you."

"That won't be necessary." He started to walk back toward his car.

"I know," she called out to him, which caused him to twist his head in her direction. "I think she'll want to."

If she wasn't mistaken, the barest trace of a smile pulled at his lips. "Then that'd be fine," he said.

She grinned and waved as he got into his car and drove off. Her gratitude for his help knew no bounds, seeing as Luke had taken off like a man on fire. She wasn't sure why. He'd been acting weirdly around her since after their dinner.

After that almost-kiss.

Had she done something wrong? She didn't know. He hadn't said.

She thought he'd been about to ask her if they could talk though. Brooke had woken up, and quite frankly, Hannah was still exhausted from everything that'd happened. Wanting to be there for her cousin, witnessing the birth of new life, forcing herself to sleep so she could take the day shift with the goats... So much needed to be done around the sanctuary, and every fiber of her being wanted to be there for it.

Mostly thanks to a man who'd opened her eyes to the magic of a town called True Love.

In the end, they'd have time to figure it out. She'd make sure of that.

But that second opinion from Text Message Guy wouldn't hurt. Plus, she wanted to set the record straight. Not just about the spinach art, but about the way he'd misread her last text.

She *definitely* wanted more moments with Luke.

Ones that ended in actual kisses. Not just almost-ones.

Hannah entered the barn to hang out with Stella for a little while. And to get some shade. True Love wasn't near Phoenix, but the summer heat still had some kick to it. Because she and Kyle had gotten the motherhood suite done themselves, she didn't need any more time in the sun.

"Hey, girl," she said to the cow. "Mind if I chill with you for a bit?"

The cow's tail swished back and forth before she lay down on a bed of hay.

"Don't mind if I do." Hannah sat next to her, leaning against her for support. "This okay?"

Stella didn't move, so Hannah took that as permission.

After adjusting a little bit, she took her phone out of her pocket and brought up Text Message Guy's thread. She reread their last few messages and memories flooded her head.

Of being so close to Luke that she could kiss him.

Of feeling his warmth just inches away from her.

Of closing her eyes and drawing nearer to him like a magnet.

Of her heart slamming in her ribs at the idea of pressing her lips to his.

Then of Ralph squeezing between them and breaking the whole scene up.

She had to laugh at it now. They'd come so close, but it just hadn't happened. There'd be time for that though, and she couldn't wait to tell him what she'd decided.

When she went back to the messages, she reviewed the last couple again.

Hannah: We just had a...moment in his kitchen. I think he almost kissed me!

Hannah: And oh my goodness, his dog broke it up, but you know what? I almost wish he hadn't.

Text Message Guy: Just tell him about your weird spinach art. Then *poof* - no more moments.

She was almost tempted to start making weird spinach art, to be honest. It was the last thing she'd ever advise one of her clients, but she'd learned a thing or two about taking chances this week. About using feelings instead of just actions. Actions got you places, but feelings could too. Feelings helped propel those actions. They were just as important.

Her fingers started to type a new message to him when Brooke poked her head into the barn.

"There you are," her cousin said. "I thought I heard you laughing in here. What's going on?'

"Oh, just the usual." Hannah let her head rest against the cow, who curled her own head back and licked Hannah's arm with her rough tongue. "Getting cow kisses and texting strangers. No big thing."

Brooke grinned as she rubbed her eyes. "Well, I'm glad things are good for you today. What's so funny?"

"Well." Hannah sat up, gave Stella a pat, and then hunched over her phone. "Yesterday, at Luke's—"

"On your date?" Brooke inquired while taking a seat next to Hannah. She stroked Stella's head with a knowing expression.

A sly grin curled the corners of Hannah's lips. "Yes, the date," she reluctantly admitted. But she also loved saying that out loud.

"She's finally figured it out," Brooke told the cow before flicking her gaze to Hannah.

Hannah waved a dismissive hand. "Yeah, yeah," she chuckled. "But does that mean you're going to figure out what's happening between you and Kyle?"

Ignoring her, Brooke continued to pet Stella instead.

"Fine," Hannah continued. "We'll avoid the topic for now, but I promise you I'm not done with that." Then she clapped her hands together to move this conversation along. "But guess what happened last night? We almost *kissed*." She whispered the last word, holding her clasped hands to her chest.

Brooke's eyebrows rose as her eyes widened. "Oh really?"

"Is that your pretend-shocked face?" Hannah deadpanned as her hands fell to her lap. "You knew that would happen!"

"Maybe now you'll stop doubting my feelings."

A warmth spread through Hannah as she picked at some hay on the barn's floor. "Yeah, maybe."

The pair stayed silent for a moment as that settled into Hannah's heart. Perhaps Brooke's feelings *were* credible, but she was blind to them for herself. That'd explain a lot.

"So," Brooke said, bringing Hannah back into the moment. "Why did that make you sit in this barn alone and laugh? And why was it 'almost kissed'?"

"Because Ralph leapt between the two of us to try to steal food off the stove. But that's not the funny part." Hannah scooted closer to her cousin and held her phone out to her. "Last night, after it happened, I texted that guy I've been chatting with this week."

"You still don't know who he is?" Brooke asked, craning her neck back to gaze at Hannah.

Hannah shook her head. "No, that's been the fun part. The anonymity has worked for us. I don't know him, he doesn't know me, so we can be...honest, I guess. There's no pressure. It's just nice to talk to him."

"But what about Luke?"

Scrunching her face, Hannah asked, "What about him?"

"I thought you liked him, not this guy you've been texting."

"I do!" The speed at which Hannah had answered nearly threw her off. She knew she'd been developing feelings for Luke, but she'd replied so quickly. "I do," she repeated more softly. "And that's what I was trying to tell Text Message Guy last night."

"To what, break it off with him?" Brooke narrowed her eyes, taking Hannah's phone from her.

Exasperated, Hannah said, "No, not like that. We've just been talking."

While Brooke scrolled, she raised a single eyebrow. "Uh, it looks like you've been flirting to me."

"That's just banter," Hannah replied, stealing her phone back. "He's funny and helpful. That's all."

"Are you sure? You're blushing."

Hannah could feel the heat on her skin, but she'd hoped that was due to a minor sunburn.

Did she have any kind of feelings for Text Message Guy? No, she didn't. Not that way, anyway. They'd been friendly. He'd been so helpful while she'd been in town. It was a happy accident, but nothing more. And she'd liked how his sense of humor reminded her of Luke in a way. She and Luke had enjoyed a similar kind of banter.

Which she'd have called flirting.

Uh oh.

Suddenly, she felt the need to set the record straight. She wanted to pursue things with Luke, no one else, now that she'd decided to stay. Telling her mystery texter was the first step toward that.

Hannah: I think you misunderstood me yesterday. I didn't mean I wanted those moments to end. Quite the opposite actually. The man I went out on a date with last night is really great, and I want to go on more dates with him. And actually kiss him next time. I like him. *Really* like him. And I think he'll accept my weird spinach art.

There. She sent that off and showed Brooke. "That's clear enough, right?"

"Well, I don't get the spinach art thing."

"It's an inside joke."

Brooke gave her a look that said *You have inside jokes with this stranger?*

But they did. Texting this guy had been so helpful from the beginning. Feeling like she could be honest and get real advice from an unbiased source had pushed her in the right direction. Perhaps she could have kept up with her old life coach after all. Instead, Text Message Guy had turned into one in a funny, playful way, and she appreciated that.

"It's pretty clear though," Brooke said. Then she set a hand on Hannah's knee. "And I'm happy for you, Han. Really happy."

"Good." Smiling to herself, she set her phone in her lap and waited for Text Message Guy's gentle understanding—along with some funny quip about her nonexistent spinach art.

That's not what she got though.

With a pinched brow, Brooke reached for Hannah's phone,

and when she turned the screen on, she brought up the text message thread. "Huh."

"What? Did he reply?" Hannah asked, leaning over to see the screen.

Brooke shook her head. "No, but I thought I saw something funny when you showed me this a moment ago."

"And?"

This time, Brooke nodded. "Yep. There it is." She pointed to the top of the thread, where *Text Message Guy* was because that's how Hannah had saved his name into her phone.

But it no longer said *Text Message Guy*.

Now, it read *Luke Steiner*.

Hannah blinked rapidly, trying to clear her eyes. Surely she was seeing things. No good reason for why Luke's name would be there on that thread of messages existed. Not one.

The only reason she could think of was: *He* was Text Message Guy.

"Why is Luke's name there? I thought you didn't know this guy." Brooke glanced back and forth between the phone and Hannah.

Hannah didn't have an answer to that. She'd thought she hadn't known him, either. But she'd had Luke save his number in her phone before he'd left the night before.

Was this some kind of joke? An accident? Were their numbers just a couple off from each other and he'd typed it in wrong?

Or was the obvious true?

Was he really Text Message Guy?

That was kind of poetic, really. She'd had a lot of fun bantering with him. He'd been a highlight of her trip, instrumental in allowing her to find things she loved about this town.

But they'd also talked about *him*. Luke. And she hadn't known who she was talking to.

She didn't want it to be true. She'd *just* fired off a message with things she hadn't been ready to tell Luke to his face. Things she'd have told him down the line, but not yet. It was way too soon to talk about "really liking" anyone after only a week—especially when that week had started off rocky, which was the nicest way to put it.

Hannah shot straight to her feet, wondering how in the world she was going to fix this. The only way she could was to go to the man himself. She'd have to face him after what she'd just sent him, but maybe she could get him to delete it before he read it. Then they'd get a good laugh that they ended up being the people they were texting this whole time and he wouldn't be the wiser.

Maybe she could save this before she screwed it all up.

18

*W*ith his head back in the game, Luke handled the morning rush like a pro. Sundays ended up being busier than during the week due to Melissa's yoga classes. So many people in town—tourists too—liked to end their weeks with yoga and juice. The health of it brought them in, and Luke was glad for it.

Plus, it kept his mind off Hannah.

By the afternoon, a steady stream of customers made for a busy day, so he barely had time to think of her. That's what he told himself anyway. Mostly, he pushed thoughts of her away and focused on what was important: his business. The one he'd completely forgotten in the middle of his personal drama.

Everything had started innocently enough, but it had with Loraine, too. Now, he felt like he was on the brink of losing everything again and things with Hannah had barely even begun. He wouldn't go there. He just wouldn't.

Except he had to when Hannah showed up at the shop at closing time looking as beautiful as ever.

Just like Brooke earlier, Hannah had hay stuck to her shorts.

Some was in her long hair, too, and he thought he saw dirt smudged on her cheek. Farm life had taken a liking to her.

It'd made Luke take a liking to her too.

His heart couldn't deny that no matter how much he wanted to.

Nervously, she intertwined her fingers, twisting them in front of her body. "Hey."

"Hey," he said back. "Here for another juice?"

She shook her head, her wide gaze fixed on him.

He braced his hands against the counter in front of him and leaned forward. "Then I should get back to work."

After glancing behind herself, she faced him again. "But there's no one in line and you're about to close up."

"And I do more than just make juices when the orders come in," he replied. Then he winced, knowing that had come out more harshly than he'd intended. "Look, I—"

"I realized I didn't give you my phone number too," she said over him, jolting forward a step. Then she paused, looking unsure of what she was about to say next. "Wanna give me your phone? I'll put it in there for you."

Though Luke wasn't quite sure what was happening, he knew without a doubt that it had something to do with the text messages they'd been sending all week. Had she figured it out? Did she know it was him now?

But more importantly: Why did it even matter?

She'd last told him through text that she wished they hadn't had that "moment" in his kitchen. All of this was one-sided, so what did *she* have to be mad about? She hadn't nearly ruined her own business because of him.

"You could have just texted me and said it was you," he said. He folded his arms over his chest and adjusted his feet to stand strong. "Why did you come all the way here for this?"

"I just—" she started, but she cut herself off. "Can I please see your phone?"

"No," he replied immediately, taking a step back. "Just text me and I'll know it's you."

Blinking, she huffed out a breath through her nose. She kept her gaze locked on his, clearly looking like she was deciding how to play this. Ultimately, she relented. "Fine."

He watched her as she tapped the message out on her phone. With a shaky finger, she pressed send and then dropped her cell back into her purse.

"There," she said. "Done."

"Thanks." As he said that, his phone beeped in the back of his shop.

After a quiet beat, she mimicked his crossed-arm stance and asked, "Gonna go save my number now?"

"I'll do it later."

"Or you could do it now." She blinked a few more times as if that would help drive him to complete her request.

Ultimately, he relented too. "Fine."

He wasn't sure how he was going to play this, either, but he'd think of something. He had to. Otherwise, not only was his business on the line, but Hannah's friendship would be too.

Mystery Woman's friendship.

He'd grown to like both Hannah and Mystery Woman. Even though he and Hannah had had a shaky start, he'd always gotten along with Mystery Woman. In some ways, he could reconcile that they were the same person now. He'd seen what was beneath Hannah's hardened exterior down to the kindness in her soul. Mystery Woman had always let that show, and their enjoyable conversations had extended into real life.

He recognized that. And he hated to lose it as soon as this unenjoyable conversation was over.

After swinging through the door to the back, he nabbed his phone off the steel counter. His heart sped in his chest as he raced through ideas of how to handle this. Nothing but his business and his past came to mind.

"If you're not going to do it," Hannah said behind him, "I will."

When he spun around, he found her in the back with him, her hand reaching forward in that same gimme motion she'd used when attempting to do the dishes at dinner. He reminded himself that he'd gotten off track, lost his vision, and nearly screwed his business up that day because of the woman standing in front of him. He'd let her cloud his judgment and forget what day it was because he'd gotten caught up in her.

So instead of giving in, he stood his ground. "No. I'll do it. Later."

"Luke, I—"

"No," he said over her. "I just can't do this right now." Then he rushed past her and hurried toward the front door to lock up.

His keys jingled as he twisted them in the lock. Then he heard the door to the back swing open, and Hannah's footsteps echoed around the small shop until her voice replaced them.

"I'm the woman you've been texting this week."

His body turned to stone, his arm frozen in midair, his fingers gripping the *open* sign to flip it. With his breath stalled in his chest, he couldn't suck any air in. This was it, where everything came crashing down.

And he was right, of course. She took his motionless silence for what it was: an admission of guilt.

"You knew," she said, her words dripping with slow awareness. "I literally just found out, but you... How long have you known?"

When he could finally pull a breath in, it felt disjointed and heavy. He could barely turn around to face her, but he knew he had to. Shame couldn't hold him back. He needed his fear and anger to push him toward what he needed to do.

"How long?" she insisted, sounding more irritated. Her cheeks flamed with pink as tears built in her eyes. "Did you read that text I sent you earlier?"

"Today?"

In tiny movements, she nodded without breaking her gaze away.

"I haven't checked my phone all day. I've been busy here." He gestured around the shop. "You know, at the business I run."

Furrowing her brow, she said, "Of course I know you run this place. That's why I'm here."

"Yeah, but you don't get it."

The creases in her forehead deepened. "What don't I get?"

His voice rose as he took a step toward her. "I almost wasn't here!" He stabbed a finger at his chest. "I forgot to be here this morning. I forgot that it was Sunday and I needed to open the shop. I forgot to put my business first."

Hannah's head jerked backward. "And that's why you didn't tell me *you* were on the other end of those texts? What does that have to do with anything?" She splayed her arms out to her sides.

"It has everything to do with what I told you yesterday about my ex-girlfriend, Hannah. I don't know what's happening between us, but it's getting in the way of my job. My livelihood. The only thing I have to my name."

"The only thing?" she questioned in a shaky voice. Then she swiped at her cheek, her emotion spilling down her skin from her eyes. "What about—" The words stopped coming, and then she changed tack, lowering her octave. "How long have you known it was me?"

His jaw tightened as his teeth clenched, but the moment he let go, the truth left his mouth. "Since last night."

Her nostrils flared as that news hit her. Several emotions radiated from her, and he couldn't land on which was most prominent. Anger? Irritation? Surprise? In the end, it didn't matter. None of them were good, and he'd need them all to do what he needed to do.

"I tried to tell you," he reasoned. "I wanted to talk to you about it, but..." He trailed off, waving a hand in the air to indicate the litany of events that had happened since dinner.

"Did you know before you tried to kiss me?" Her voice was deadly calm. Steady now. But her fists were clamped tight.

He sucked in a breath to tell her no, he didn't know before that. But quite frankly, he'd had his suspicions. And that pause before answering seemed to give her everything she needed to know.

Her scoff hit him straight in the heart. "How could you?" Another tear fell in a fiery path down her cheek. "You pretended not to know when you replied about spinach art, and then you misunderst—never mind." She threw her arms into the air and brushed past him for the door.

He'd locked it though, so she bounced off it instead of going through it.

But something she'd said piqued his interest.

"I misunderstood?"

"Unlock this door," she seethed through gritted teeth. Staying pressed up against the door, she refused to face him.

So he stared burning holes into the back of her head as he spoke. "What did I misunderstand, Hannah?"

"Just open the door, Luke. This conversation is over." She jiggled the door as if that'd magically unlock it.

He wanted to hear her say it. A twisted part of him wanted to know for sure that he'd misread her text and she *did* in fact want more of those moments. He needed to know what he was giving up in order to save his business. "Tell me."

She shook her head, not giving the information up.

After a step forward, he tried again. "Tell me what I misunderstood."

When she said nothing, he got closer to her. A few moments later, his breath fanned her adorably mussed hair as he spoke.

"Hannah. What did I misunderstand?"

A shiver ran down her spine before she gulped. "It doesn't matter. You betrayed my trust. That's not okay."

"And I nearly tanked my business today because I was falling in—" He shut up before something he couldn't unsay left his lips.

At that, she spun right around. Watery, red eyes stared up at him. "You were what?" It wasn't a question so much as a statement. A way to mock how he'd been asking for information a few moments earlier. "You were what, Luke? Say it. Tell me."

He ground his teeth to keep the words back. It'd only been a week. It was insane to think he was feeling that way, but his heart ached, stamping every inch of that truth throughout his body each time it beat.

For her.

Shaking his head, he retreated away from her. "No."

"Tell me. You were falling in what?"

This time, he didn't answer her. He didn't even move, save for his Adam's apple, which bobbled with his hard swallow.

She released a breath from her nose, and he could feel the disappointment spreading throughout the room. "I am *not* Loraine. I never would have made you choose between me and your business, and if you didn't see that, then I don't know what to tell you."

Oh, he knew she wasn't Loraine, all right. She was *more*. He'd known it from the moment she'd spit her fire his way. He'd been addicted from the start, and he should have seen this coming. A woman like Hannah didn't make a guy fall in love. She made a guy fall to pieces when she chewed him up and spit him out. He'd have time to recover when she was back in Vermont, but for now...

It had to end.

Before history repeated itself and it was too late for him.

Though that little voice in the back of his head told him that it already was.

He stepped forward again, leaving her just a breath away from his lips again. Just like the night before, the only thing he wanted to do was close that distance between them and seal his mouth over hers. He could make this whole thing go away with a kiss. Maybe then he'd see that there were no sparks, no fireworks between them. Maybe.

In that moment, he desperately wanted to know what kissing her felt like, if it'd turn out to be nothing or everything he thought it'd be: heaven on Earth, a lifetime of banter-filled texts, and hikes in all of his favorite spots rolled into one.

He didn't need to perform the act in order to know.

It'd be all of that.

And more.

So, instead of doing the one thing he wanted more than his next breath, he slipped his keys from his pocket and unlocked the door.

As he stared into her eyes, he thought he saw shock pass over them. Maybe even hurt. Had she really expected something else? Had she thought they'd be able to get past this? After he'd told her that this exact situation could never happen, he wasn't sure why she'd think that.

But he swore he witnessed it anyway.

Then it was gone, replaced with that anger he knew she was capable of.

"Do me one last favor," she told him, disdain falling off every word. "Delete the text I sent today. Or read it if you want. And then pretend like it never existed because I don't mean it anymore."

Then he watched the woman of his dreams slip out the exit and his world shattered at his feet.

19

"Wow," Hannah said. "I can't believe how far we've come in the last two weeks."

"It's my labor of love," Brooke cooed as they both watched the knobby-kneed baby goat stumble over to his mother. Then she gave Hannah a side-eyed look as she brushed her bangs out of her eyes. "It could be *our* labor of love, you know. I need a caretaker here. You don't *have* to leave."

Hannah dipped her head and glared at her cousin. "You know why I'm going." Then she pulled her phone out and requested a rideshare to take her to Flagstaff so she could catch a flight to Phoenix and then another to Vermont.

Sighing, Brooke made her way back toward the tiny home. "I know why you *say* you're going. I just don't think it's a valid reason."

"I'm going because I have a ticket for today with my name on it," Hannah reminded her as she went through the front door. Her suitcase was already packed—had been since Monday when she'd tried to leave on standby. But no available seats and a three-hundred-dollar fee to purchase a new one sooner than her originally scheduled flight meant she'd come back to True Love with her tail between her legs. "Finally."

"Oh, come on, Han." Brooke propped her shoulder against the doorjamb and crossed her arms over her chest. "It's not that bad. Really. You don't have to avoid him forever."

"Of course I don't have to. And I couldn't," Hannah insisted. "It's been hard enough trying to for the last week in a town this small. Forever would be torture."

"Or," her cousin said, drawing the word out for several seconds, "you could just apologize like you want to and move on. Things don't have to be awkward or weird."

"No, they don't have to be, but they are. That's all there is to it."

Brooke pushed off the door and curled up in the chair as Hannah stuck her sunglasses on her head. "So then stay here. We'll build you another tiny home right next to mine and you can help with the sanctuary. You never have to leave and it'll be perfect!" She clasped her hands together and let a big, cheesy grin loose.

Hannah hated to let her cousin down, but she'd done what she'd gone there to do: help out with the sanctuary. She'd offered up physical labor, and in the last week, she'd done the mental kind, brainstorming ways to raise funds for future pens or barn construction and the general upkeep of the place. They'd taken on way more animals than Brooke had planned on, and each mouth needed to be fed. Plus, with cooler months coming up, Brooke would need all the money she could get her hands on to keep everyone warm and happy.

"Not when I can go back home to my regular-sized house ten minutes from a Whole Foods, put thousands of miles between me and he-who-shall-not-be-named, and help you over the internet with less manual labor involved." Hannah returned her own cheesy grin, though it didn't reach her eyes.

Because, if she were being truthful, she didn't want to go.

"But then how could you snuggle the new babies?" Brooke asked. "You can't do that if you're on the East Coast, can you?"

Hannah leaned against the small oven across from the chair Brooke was in. "No, but I could focus on finding clients who actually need my help again."

In the two weeks since she'd let everyone know she'd be on vacation, they all seemed to have decided that she'd done her job *too* well. Every single one of her regular clients felt well-adjusted enough not to need her on a weekly basis. They'd opted to keep the lines of communication open in case they had a problem, but Lucy's email to her had summarized it pretty succinctly.

From: lucy.harden1@email.com

To: hannah@hannahlockhartcoach.com

Subject: Re: Coaching

*Hey, Hannah! Thanks for getting back to me so quickly, and I'm sorry it's taken me so long to reply, but it's for a good reason. I made a decision, stuck with it, and got **FOUR** new leads because of it. That has never happened before, and I have you to thank for it all! Life has really turned around because of you. I can't say thank you enough.*

I hope your vacation has been amazing. Maybe you'll come back feeling refreshed and ready to take on life the way I am now.

If anything new comes up, I'll email you if that's okay? I think that'll be a good way for me to feel still in control but not feel like I need you as a crutch – something else I've learned from you!

Thanks again!

Lucy

Hannah had wanted to both cry tears of joy for Lucy and scream because of that email. Her client had obtained the ultimate goal, after all. But Hannah was left with one fewer client to work with. Then, when a dozen emails just like that one had come in, that total had dropped to a level she hadn't seen in years.

So, now, it was time for her to get back home and find new ones.

"Look," Brooke said, filtering inside Hannah's internal thoughts, "the way I see it is you have some time on your hands right now. Maybe that's time you need to spend on yourself." Quickly, she added more before Hannah defended that. "That does *not* mean you need to include he-who-shall-not-be-named in that time. That's completely up to you. But it sounds to me like you don't need to find new coaching clients. The perfect client for you to coach through life is right here in this room."

Hannah blinked rapidly at her cousin. "You know I don't work with family."

"No!" Brooke laughed as she rose from her chair. It took half a step before she was in front of Hannah, placing her hands on her shoulders. "Not me. You."

That gave Hannah pause. Of course she knew that her life wasn't perfect. She had plenty of faults and things to work on. But she'd been trained to manage them for her clients, not herself. Still, from time to time, she used the techniques she asked her clients to try out, and they usually worked. However, not every situation had a clear-cut solution.

Right then, she found herself in the middle of one of those.

"Think about it." Brooke opened the door and stepped out into the afternoon sunshine. "You could stay here, do as little manual labor as you want, and maybe still try to find some online coaching clients if you want. But I think this mini life vacation has done you some good, so it might be time to embrace that."

Hannah met her on the porch and gripped the railing as she peered over the emerald-green grass. She watched Stella head into her barn to find some shade and three goats huddle around the baby when he wobbled on his seven-day-old legs. Then one of the pigs got the zoomies, taking off at a dead sprint from one side of the pen to the other. Its curly tail bobbled while its little legs tore up ground.

It brought so much warmth to her heart.

There was so much life there at the sanctuary. So many moments she'd miss, memories she'd never have, and experiences she'd never get anywhere else.

It wasn't a bad idea. But...

"That doesn't help me with the other problem, Brooke. This town is the size of a postage stamp. I wouldn't be able to never see Luke again."

Brooke gazed at Hannah, but she ignored it. "Seems to me like you're coming around already if you're able to say his name again."

She wouldn't admit it to Brooke, but she'd never truly stopped. Not in her head anyway. Not when she'd written up countless text message drafts that had ultimately ended up in the digital trash. Not when she'd wrestled with the entire situation in her head. And especially not when she'd realized she'd overreacted in a big way.

Hannah had blamed him for breaking their trust. For not coming to her sooner once he'd figured out who she was.

But he had.

Yes, he'd asked to talk to her. Yes, she'd told him that it'd have to be later. Yes, he'd left before they could have that talk.

Yet the night before, she'd asked for his phone number and he'd given it to her.

He'd known full well what would happen when she pulled his text message thread up the next time.

He'd given her all the information she'd needed. It'd just taken her too long to put it together.

That didn't absolve him completely, but it made her regret

how angry she'd been. How she'd told him to forget that last message she'd sent him. How she'd said she didn't mean it anymore.

Her heart reminded her every day that she'd lied through her teeth.

She'd been hurt, yes. Incredibly hurt that he'd felt similarly about her but hadn't given her the opportunity to show him she wasn't his ex-girlfriend. That she'd never, not in a million years, make him choose between her or his business. She'd never put his job in jeopardy—quite the opposite, actually. She had years of experience helping people grow their businesses. That was part of what she did for a living, and she could have done that for him too.

If he'd let her. But he hadn't.

Sighing, Hannah squeezed her fingers around the porch railing and then let go. "Is this about the 'feeling' you had when I got here?"

"It might be," Brooke said. "But my feelings don't mean anything without action behind them."

Hannah felt the truth of those words in her soul. She'd thought as much just a week earlier when she'd begun giving credence to Brooke's feelings. Her cousin had been right about this one, after all.

"What about when you were wrong about Teddy? Are we ever going to talk about that?" Hannah twisted her head toward Brooke.

"Another time," Brooke promised. "Right now, this is about you."

"So we're also not going to talk about what's going on with you and Kyle?"

Brooke's cheeks grew red. "Only if you want to talk about you and Luke."

Hannah scrunched her face, but a smile she couldn't help

formed on her lips. Something was going on there, and she wanted to stick around to find out.

"That's what I thought," Brooke said, a matching expression on her face.

After pulling in a deep breath, Hannah let it out. She'd come to appreciate the fresh mountain air in True Love. The people there. All the hiking trails, and even Carrie Ann's Diner. She'd met the woman behind the place herself, along with her husband, Norman. They were great people, and she'd finally come to understand why everyone loved that place so much.

It wasn't about the food as much as it was about the people who ran it. Good, decent, kind people who cared about the community.

Just like Luke did.

Hannah understood that now that she'd given herself the space to think about it.

Turned out there was a ton of time to think when days were spent feeding animals, shoveling manure, and helping Misty and Brooke in the garden they'd gotten started. *So* much time to think.

And that's what propelled her to the rideshare car that had just shown up.

"Uh," Brooke said while Hannah bounded down the steps. "Aren't you forgetting something?"

Hannah paused, thinking about that. "Oh!" Then she spun around, marched up the two stairs, and gave her cousin a big hug.

"Don't you need your suitcase?"

"I would if I were leaving," Hannah said before heading back toward the lot. She waved at the driver, who stayed inside the car.

Brooke's eyes went wide as saucers and she clapped her hands. "Does that mean you're staying?"

"It depends," Hannah answered, which made Brooke deflate a little—only a little. "I do need to talk about Luke if I'm going to stay here." Before her cousin could get too excited, she rushed to add, "But only *to* Luke. So...I'll be right back."

Brooke's wide eyes lit with delight, and her voice chased Hannah as she strode across the grass to the car. "Hey, Hannah?"

Just before she opened the car door, she tilted her head toward her cousin. "Yeah?"

As Brooke swept some of her pixie cut out of her face, she said, "I have a really good feeling about this."

Even though Hannah hadn't believed in all of that before, her heart soared. Brooke's good feelings meant a lot to her now.

And she hoped against hope that this one came true.

20

*L*uke's heart ached. Hard.

It'd been a whole week since Luke had closed the shop after Hannah had left. He didn't want those memories to race across the backs of his eyes while he locked up, but they did. Memories of the last time he'd ever be that close to her—because he was sure he'd lost any chance of doing that again.

Instead, he'd thrown himself into his work and caring for Ralph. He made sure to check the schedule with Mateo several times and even put it in his Google calendar with alerts.

If he'd lost the girl, he wouldn't lose his business on top of that.

It'd all been his fault though. He'd pushed her away, given her no choice but to go. He'd held back in telling her the truth instead of insisting they talk to get that cleared up. He'd forgotten what day it was, not her. And he'd kept his true feelings to himself even when she'd asked a couple of times.

Especially after he'd read the text she'd requested he delete and forget forever.

Yeah. Right.

Never going to happen.

Luke hadn't had it in him to do any of those things she'd asked him to do. In fact, now that the shop was closed and quiet, he pulled his phone from his pocket and walked over to one of the small tables for two. After placing the back of the chair against the table, he sat, propped one elbow on the table, and put his head in his hand. Then he brought up their text message thread and read that message one more time.

Just to drive the arrow through his chest a little more.

Hannah: I think you misunderstood me yesterday. I didn't mean I wanted those moments to end. Quite the opposite actually. The man I went out on a date with last night is really great, and I want to go on more dates with him. And actually kiss him next time. I like him. *Really* like him. And I think he'll accept my weird spinach art.

He would have. If she'd been into spinach art, he truly would have been the first in line to buy it. He would have kissed her any time she wanted and taken her wherever she'd have liked to go on a date. He'd have made boiled dinner every single day for the rest of their lives if that's what she'd have wanted.

Like an idiot, he'd fallen in love.

And like a bigger idiot, he'd pushed her away.

He knew that now, but there was nothing he could do to make that up to her. It was the only thing he wanted to do now. Not run his business. Not make smoothies for tourists.

He just wanted Hannah back.

Sighing, he hung his head

If he'd have realized that sooner, he wouldn't have been in those shoes. But there he was and he'd have to deal with it.

Or...

He had her number, after all. He knew for sure it was her. How would she respond if he sent her a text? How would she feel about that?

Or would she not respond at all?

With some time between events, he thought maybe she'd cooled down. She was probably back home already anyway, so there was no pressure. If he hadn't seen her in town in the last week, she couldn't still be there. So if he did text her now, he wouldn't run into her and have to make awkward small talk about the weather. Or ask if she'd been to Carrie Ann's lately. Or pretend like he didn't still love her.

It'd be fine.

Right?

He wouldn't know unless he tried, so he adjusted his backwards baseball cap and gave it his best shot.

Luke: Maybe I shouldn't send this, but I want you to know that I'm sorry. We've been known to apologize a time or two, so here I am, doing it again. I hope you can forgive me.

To his utter shock, a response came in right away.

Hannah: Good thing my spinach art is ready so you can make it up to me.

With a tremble in his fingers, he brought his phone closer to his face to read that message. Sitting up straighter, he read it again, wondering if that actually meant he could get a second chance.

Luke: Name your price.

Hannah: Does that mean business is good? I wouldn't want to threaten your livelihood or anything.

He wasn't sure if he should laugh or let that push the arrow in deeper to cause more pain.

Luke: That was fair. I earned that. But let's just say that business isn't as fulfilling as I thought it'd be now that you're gone.

Hannah: Hmm. Who said I was gone?

He whipped his gaze to the door, not expecting to see her there. It was just instinct, a hope that she really hadn't left town.

But there she was, right outside the glass—the woman of his dreams.

With sunglasses perched on top of her head and her long locks floating over her shoulders, she didn't look anything like the woman who'd shown up a week before. No hay could be found on her clothes, no dirt on her cheeks, and most importantly, no tears in her eyes.

Though he couldn't be sure of what he was seeing in them now, he knew one thing for certain: It wasn't sadness.

It could have been humor. Perhaps optimism, but that could have been him seeing what he wanted to see. What he wanted to see in her eyes was hope. Trust. Love.

Not that he deserved any of those things, but still. A guy could ask anyway.

He crept over to the door as if he weren't sure she was real. If he hadn't received those texts, he would have thought he was imagining things. She was really there though.

Still in True Love.

But was she still in...

No. She'd never said that. He'd been the only one to almost go there. All she'd said to him when she'd thought they were anonymous was that she *really* liked him. That wasn't love. And she'd told him to forget she'd ever written those words, so the answer was no.

His keys jangled as he unlocked the door and opened it for her. Tentatively, she entered his shop, her lips pulled into a tight line that gave nothing away.

"What are you doing here?" he dared to ask, his voice barely above a whisper.

"Well," she said, slipping her hands into her pockets, "someone said he wanted to apologize. I'm all ears."

He watched her for a moment, quietly taking her in. Her stance was strong, her posture resilient—just like her. Of course she'd stuck it out and been fine. That's who Hannah was as a person, and he should have expected nothing less.

He shook his head. "Not until someone coughs up their spinach art." He held a hand out, palm up.

That made her break into a breathtaking grin that nearly made his heart stop. He hadn't thought he'd ever see that again, so to have it happen now, before his very eyes... He almost couldn't take it.

She ducked her gaze before the expression fell and she went serious again. "Actually, Luke, I need to apologize too."

Intrigued, he raised his eyebrows. "Oh?"

"Yeah. I..." She tucked some of her loose hair behind her ear and then took a deep breath. "I shouldn't have been so mad about...that. You knowing that it was me on the phone. You did try to tell me."

"I know," he said, "but I could have told you sooner."

"You did though," she insisted, stepping forward. "When you gave me your number, you had to have known I'd notice eventually. Maybe not right away, but when we texted next. Though..." She chuckled, but he wasn't sure why. "I almost didn't, actually. Brooke had to point it out." Then she laughed again. "And that was after she asked about spinach art, which was hard to explain because it was an inside joke. Then she wondered why I had an inside joke with Text Message Guy, and I—"

"Text Message Guy?" He couldn't help but question that. It was too good.

She tilted her head, keeping her gaze aimed at him almost defiantly, which was cute. "Well, yeah. What did you call me?"

He pressed his lips together, not quite wanting to admit it. But the humor of the situation was getting to him. "Mystery Woman," he mumbled.

Her eyes flared as she held another laugh back. "So much better," she sassed.

"Anyway," he said, stretching the word out around his grin. "Keep going. You were talking with Brooke."

"Oh, right. So, she didn't understand why I had an inside joke with...well, you, but it was because we were kind of friends that way. Texting with you was..." She trailed off, searching all around the shop for the right word.

He provided her with one when she couldn't seem to find it. "Perfect?"

When her gaze finally landed on him again, she nodded. "Yeah. It was, wasn't it?"

"It was," he agreed, his voice low. He wasn't sure where she was going with this, but admitting that was the first step to getting crushed again. "But what does that have to do with this?"

"Everything," she insisted, her hands open out to her sides. "Don't you see? It has everything to do with this. Because the whole time, all of the fun banter—"

"You mean flirting?"

She gave him a stern look full of humor and impatience. "The texting, Luke. Our back-and-forth. It was fun. Playful. Maybe even addicting."

He spoke up when she was quiet for too long. "And?"

"And..." She filled her chest with air and took another step in his direction. "And it was always us."

His face pinched as he thought about that. "I'm not sure I'm following."

"All it did was make me realize that we get along so much better than I thought we did. At first, we had a rough go of it, snapping a little in stressful situations," she said, and she wasn't wrong, he thought. "And then we started texting without knowing each other, so I felt like I got to know the real you. The person you are deep down when no one is watching. The guy who helps out of the kindness of his heart because he cares about people, his community, and his dog so much." A watery chuckle made her last word wobbly. Tears balanced on her lids, but she didn't move to wipe them away.

"That's exactly the guy I want to be," he said. "But that's not who I've felt like this last week."

"But that's who you are," she said, looking confused.

Sadly, he hung his head and shook it. Then he raised it again and aimed his eyes right at her. "That's who I am with *you*."

She gasped, but the sound was quiet, muffled by her fingertips placed gently against her lips.

"I mean, don't get me wrong." Smirking a little to lighten the mood, he adjusted his baseball cap. "I'm that guy. I offer up suggestions of hiking trails to strangers. Heck"—he tossed his arms out to his sides and let them fall against his thighs—"I keep opening juice shops to provide healthy options for the people in my community and put that first instead of..." His voice cut out as he closed that part of himself off.

So Hannah finished for him. "Instead of allowing yourself to explore other opportunities? Instead of realizing it doesn't have to be one or the other?" Two steps later, she was close enough for him to touch.

He kept his hands to himself even though they itched to run through her hair. "Yeah. That."

"Luke, I was never going to make you choose. I need you to know that."

Guilt swept over him, and he tried to swallow over the knot building in his throat. "I know that now. I wasn't going to let you, but I didn't even give you the chance."

"If you'd heard me out," she said, a knowing grin forming on her mouth, "you'd know that I actually help people build their businesses. Professionally, that's what I do as part of life coaching."

"I know," he answered, having the decency to look sheepish.

She crinkled her forehead. "You do?"

Along with oxygen, he took in the courage he needed to admit this next bit. "I might have Googled you since last week."

Hannah's face relaxed as a pleasantly surprised expression filled it. "So you've been thinking about me."

"Well." He put his hands on his hips and gazed at her through his eyelashes. "I was actually thinking about Mystery Woman."

She broke into laughter over that, which was contagious to him. Music to his ears, really. He'd gone from thinking he'd never see her again to having her right there in his shop, within touching distance as she laughed at one of his jokes.

When a heavy silence settled over them, Luke decided to be the one to break it with his truth. With a hand on the back of his neck, he dove in. "I've been, in a word, miserable since last weekend. At first, it was because I was worried about my shop. I let things get in my way with the last one, and I'd vowed never to do that again."

"I know," she told him.

"But you don't know everything." He let his hand fall. "You don't know that I didn't feel half as horrible when Loraine left as I did when you left. You don't know that I've checked my phone a thousand times, hoping you'd text me again. You don't know that I've wished I could have realized I'd be more upset about losing you than this place before I actually lost you. And you don't know that I read that text you said I shouldn't. The one you told me to delete."

Hannah bit her lip, staring at him without words.

"I know you told me not to read it, but I had to," he told her earnestly. "It was the last communication I thought I'd have with you, so I needed it. And all one thousand of those times I checked my phone, hoping to see a new one, that old one broke my heart."

The grip she had on her lip with her teeth tightened. He

worried she might start bleeding soon, so he did something he didn't think he should do.

He put his thumb against her lip and cupped her cheek with his palm. "When Loraine asked the impossible of me, I couldn't do it. But if you asked me right now to choose, I'd do it. In a heartbeat, Hannah." He brushed her other cheek with his knuckles before his hands slipped into her hair. "The beauty of it is that you'd never make me, but I'd choose you."

Her breath caught, and she opened her mouth to say something but closed it when nothing came out.

The corners of his lips twitched. "Did I make Hannah Lockhart speechless?" he joked.

When her jaw fell open, she playfully scoffed. "I guess you did. For once in my life, I have no witty comeback." Then she softened and said, "That was really beautiful, Luke. Thanks for recognizing that."

He had nothing more to say, either. No witty comeback of his own. No flirty banter as a response. All he wanted to do was the one thing he'd tried to do before. With no Ralph in sight, he saw no obstacles in his way, so he leaned in and—

"Wait!" she whisper-shouted, moving her head back a bit. "I realized something."

"That spinach art is never gonna be a thing?" he asked, trying to slow his racing heart. He'd been *so* close.

"No," she chuckled. "If anyone is going to make it a thing, it'll be me."

He didn't doubt that. But he was doubting his patience to finally kiss this woman. "What did you realize, then?"

"That, when we were texting, you said your dog was sick." Her expression turned sad. "Is Ralph okay?"

"Oh." He gazed toward the ground, and his heart pinched. "Yeah, I don't know. He has an appointment in a week to have x-rays done, but the vet is hopeful."

"Can I come?"

"To the appointment?" he asked. Hope fluttered in his chest. She nodded.

"That'd be really great. And I'm sure Ralph would love it."

Her lips softly curved up. "Good. Know what else?"

He knew what he wanted. But if he didn't ask, they'd never get there. "What?"

She walked over to the bell on the counter and made it ring out. The sly, open, free expression on her face made his heart race against his ribs. "I know what I want now."

As he followed her over there, he recalled the moment he told her to do that. She'd just entered his shop for the first time, and even though he'd recognized how beautiful she was, he'd been a jerk. Still, there they were, with a deeper understanding of who they were as people now, and he desperately wanted to know more about her.

"What's that?" he asked, standing right in front of Hannah.

Instead of answering with words, she answered with an action: pressing her lips to his to finally, *finally*, kiss.

It was everything he'd hoped it'd be.

And more.

Heaven on Earth and then some.

Luke's lips tingled as he deepened the kiss. Her soft hair tickled his fingers when he ran them against her scalp. As he leaned in closer, she did too, wrapping her arms around his middle and squeezing like she never wanted to let him go.

He hoped she didn't.

"Hey," she said, breaking their first kiss way too soon. Her expression said that she knew she was teasing him—and she liked it. "There's one more thing I want."

He fought an eye roll full of playfulness. With Hannah, he knew what he was getting into, but she never ceased to amaze him anyway. "What more could you want than this?" He let his hands settle at the base of her spine and clasped them there, holding her to him. Then he raised his eyebrows, daring her to challenge him.

But he knew she would.

"Well…" She trailed off, leaning away to place her hands on his chest. "Someone told me they had a lot more hiking suggestions, but that guy stopped messaging me. Since I'll be here for a while, I don't suppose you know anyone who might be able to fill his shoes and show me around?" She tilted her head, giving him a mischievous smirk.

He let out a light chuckle before readjusting his fingers behind her back. "I might know someone who can help you out. I'll have him send you a text."

Her grin made warmth spread throughout his chest. He'd do a lot of things to have that smile aimed at him for the rest of his life. Like admit right there in the place where it all started for them how he felt about her.

"In the interest of full disclosure," he said, "so you can't get mad that I didn't tell you soon enough this time, I should tell you that…" With one hand, he smoothed some of her hair out of her face and then cupped her cheek. "I love you, Hannah."

She didn't even miss a beat. "My weird spinach art and all?"

He beamed a happy expression her way. "Especially your weird spinach art."

This time, she pressed up onto her toes and kissed him, and it was more spectacular than the first time around. He wanted to continue the theory that each one would get better and better, but she had other plans.

"I love you too, Luke," Hannah whispered against his lips. "And Ralph, and this shop, and this town. I love it all, and I want it to be my new home."

Luke lit up in a way he never had before. With Hannah at his side, his future looked bigger, brighter, and better than it ever had. He'd show her how much she meant to him, and she'd stay there in town and be with him and Ralph. She might never know how happy that made him, but he'd spend the rest of his life showing her.

Hannah.

The woman of his dreams.

His new main squeeze.

Forever.

EPILOGUE

*H*annah squeezed Luke's hand as they entered the vet's office. "It's going to be fine," she reassured him. "Brooke told me she had a good feeling about this."

"You take stock in her feelings now?" Luke asked, sounding a little shocked while he ushered Ralph inside.

"She was right about you, wasn't she?" She winked at him before taking a seat in the waiting room.

She hadn't asked to come along to this appointment for Ralph's sake. She was pretty sure the dog was fine too. He had even more spunk than he'd had when she'd met him. But she knew that Luke would feel better when the doctor gave Ralph the all clear.

Plus, she had someone to meet.

Hannah patiently waited until the woman who ran the front desk returned from the back. She had a tight, gray bun secured at the nape of her neck, and much to Hannah's amusement, she looked nothing like the man she'd accidentally texted three weeks ago.

"Hey, Luke," Sylvia said before waving to Ralph. "Dr. Stevens will see you in just a bit."

"Thanks." He looped Ralph's leash around his palm.

Sylvia's gaze slid to Hannah, who waved at the woman. Then Sylvia hushed her voice, but Hannah still heard her. "Who's the pretty lady back there?" She wagged her eyebrows at Luke.

Hannah had to hold her laughter in.

"Actually," Luke said, "that's a funny story."

At that, Hannah approached the desk and explained that Misty had accidentally written Luke's number down instead of hers. While helping plant vegetables in the garden on a morning Luke had off from the shop, they'd all found it hilarious.

Hannah had laughed, but she'd counted her lucky stars too.

That wasn't something that happened often. If ever.

And feelings hadn't gotten her there. Actions had.

But feelings had grown from those actions, and she *did* put stock in that now. The proof was in the pudding, and she couldn't deny that.

"Oh wow!" Sylvia crowed. "I've never been more thankful that someone got my number wrong. Although"—she partitioned her mouth off as if it'd keep Luke from hearing—"I probably have better trail recommendations than this guy." With her free hand, she pointed at him and then winked at Hannah.

"I heard that," Luke called out, but he was hardly complaining. That happy expression on his face made Hannah think he didn't care at all if she took those suggestions.

As long as she was there with him.

It's where she planned to stay for a long time.

Brooke was ecstatic. When Hannah had returned with Luke by her side, she'd squealed her delight, barely having enough energy left over for her "I told you so" speech. She'd let Brooke say it all she wanted though. She couldn't care less if she'd been wrong now that they'd cleared the air.

Hannah was still looking for a place to stay, but everyone would keep their eyes open for an apartment or a home to rent.

Real estate was a hot commodity in True Love, which was partly why Brooke had built her house on the sanctuary's property. No one wanted to leave the small mountain town, and Hannah now openly admitted that she could see exactly why.

Everyone there was kind, compassionate, and caring.

And it somehow knew who to pair up so they'd find their own true love.

It'd happened to Hannah, so she fully believed in the legend of this town. She hoped to witness more of its magic throughout her years there too.

Perhaps even with Brooke and Kyle. Time would tell.

The only piece of the puzzle that was missing was Ralph's diagnosis. Hannah knew how much Luke had been stressing out about it, but Hannah had helped ease his mind by keeping Ralph at the sanctuary all day with her. The dog would come running to Brooke's home when it was mealtime, but other than that, he spent most of the day out in the barn, always a stone's throw away from Stella.

Stella didn't even seem to mind. In fact, Hannah thought they were True Love's newest couple.

The town didn't discriminate. Human, dog, or cow— everyone found their soul mate.

Hannah was a nervous nelly when Dr. Stevens showed them into the exam room. It got worse for Luke when she took Ralph in for his x-rays, so Hannah held his hand and gently reminded him that they could do all the spinach art he wanted after this.

He readily agreed, eager to find out what the heck that was.

She had no idea, but she'd make anything in the world up to take his mind off something he couldn't control.

Luckily, Dr. Stevens came back with great news. "He looks healthier than he was before the valley fever, Luke. Really, I think Ralph is going to be fine for a long time to come."

With tears in his eyes, he clutched Hannah around her waist, squeezing her to him. He kissed her temple, not needing to say anything for her to know what he was feeling.

Relief.

Joy.

Love.

Maybe Brooke was rubbing off on her. Just a little bit.

Luke gave Ralph all the head scratches on the way to the car. "Hear that, bud? You're doing great."

"Yep," Hannah said when she reached the passenger's door. "Stella will be excited too. Think we should head there so we can tell her?"

"As long as we can make boiled dinner at your cousin's place," he answered, unlocking the car with the fob and letting Ralph get into the back seat.

Hannah fought an eye roll. "You really don't have to keep making that. Seriously, I'm not homesick. Just sick of eating the same vegetables every night."

He feigned a gasp as if she'd wounded him. "I thought you loved the way I cook that."

"I did. The first three times. Now, we have enough left over to feed the entire town." She went to open her door, thinking that that wasn't an exaggeration.

But he pressed the door closed and boxed her in against it with his arms. "Then what would you like to eat tonight?" he asked, his voice growing low and husky. "I make a mean smoothie, but other than that, it's boiled dinner."

Her stomach filled with butterflies as he leaned in. It didn't matter how many times they'd kissed since that first one. Each one gave her tingles all the way down to her toes.

She pushed up onto the balls of her feet to get closer, closing her eyes as she prepared to kiss Luke again. Her heart fluttered in anticipation, and her knees grew weaker the closer she got.

But the sound of Ralph's loud, impatient bark caused them to jump apart right before it happened.

"Ralph!" Luke groaned around a laugh. "Come on, buddy. We've had this talk."

Hannah giggled too, though she wasn't going to let Ralph win this one. She loved that dog something fierce—kind of like how she loved Luke—but kissing him was at the top of her pro column, so she'd make sure it happened.

She rose back up onto her toes, cupped his scruffy cheeks, and kissed her true love's full, soft lips right there at the corner of Heart and Soul.

The place where her heart would always live and her soul would always thrive.

In True Love, Arizona.

Her brand-new home.

TO THE READER

Thank you for picking this book up. I know you have a lot to choose from out there, and I might be unknown to you. So I can't tell you how much it means to me that you've chosen this one. I truly hope you've enjoyed it.

I fell in love while creating the town of True Love. I also love animals so much, so it was only natural to marry the two. That's how this series was born, and I look forward to writing more love stories at the True Love Animal Sanctuary! Hopefully you're looking forward to reading more of them too.

I don't have a full plan on how often I'll releases these. But if you're signed up for my newsletter, you'll get alerts for when new ones are coming out. I just knew I had to get Hannah and Luke's story out there, but more are coming - especially Brooke and Kyle's. Don't worry. Trust me. It's coming! :)

See you there!
-EB

ACKNOWLEDGMENTS

This is yet another book, the start of a new series, that I couldn't have put together without my team!

Even though my husband thinks this town's name is a little cheesy, he's always rooting for my success - and not because my success is his. He believes in me more than anyone else, and I'm so thankful for every opportunity I get to make our dreams come true. Love you!

My proofreader, Lisa Lee - you are incredible! You fit me into your schedule so seamlessly and do such great work for me. Thank you so, so much. :)

Kellie and Kat have been so supportive of this idea since I told them about it over a year and a half ago. This series is a long time coming, and I've only gotten this far because of their encouragement and daily sprints. Thanks, ladies!

My ARC readers and eagle-eyed proofreaders are my backbone! This book wouldn't be what it is without their careful reading and sweet reviews that help others trust buying my books. Thanks so much. :)

To my FB group and my newsletter subscribers, thanks for sticking with me! It's been such a dream come true to have so many people supporting me. I can't thank you enough.

And another big thank-you shout-out to the sweet authors who've promoted me in their newsletters. This series wouldn't launch quite so well without your help. Thank you!

ABOUT THE AUTHOR

Eliza Boyd is a sweet contemporary romance author. Born and raised in Northern Illinois, she now lives in sunny Arizona with her husband and her plethora of animals. When she's not reading, writing, or working, she can be found walking around her neighborhood (for exercise, not for stalking), taking photos of her pets, or catching up on her favorite shows. Catching up really means binge-watching.

Get a FREE novella by going to elizaboydwrites.com.

facebook.com/authorelizaboyd

twitter.com/elizaboydwrites

instagram.com/elizaboydwrites

amazon.com/author/elizaboyd

bookbub.com/profile/eliza-boyd

goodreads.com/elizaboydwrites

Made in the USA
Middletown, DE
05 February 2022

60573415R00106